# MYSTERY MEN
## (& WOMEN)

AIRSHIP 27 PRODUCTIONS

Mystery Men (& Women) Volume Three

An Airship 27 Production
www.airship27.com
www.airship27hangar.com

Editor: Ron Fortier
Associate Editor: Charles Saunders
Production and design by Rob Davis.

ISBN-13: 978-0615725994
ISBN-10: 0615725996

Printed in the United States of America

10 9 8 7 6 5 4 3 2 1

# MYSTERY MEN
## (&WOMEN) VOLUME 3
### -Table of Contents-

# THE SKEIN

## *"The Swamp Chiller"*
### By Kevin Noel Olson

Stitcher Gleaves, son of the proprietor Joe Gleaves of Gleaves Place, Tavern and Mortuary, played the piano to an empty barroom. He sang with a voice deep and rich as he struck the piano keys in perfect time.

"My living," Stitcher sang, "is mine–that's what I said. 'Cause living's nobody's business but the living dead's."

The fingers ceased playing the piano abruptly. A sudden chill came over the back of Stitcher's neck. His smile fell. He closed the keyboard cover. He pushed his bowler hat back.

Thinly, a voice whispered from behind him, "Don't turn around Jacob Moses Gleaves."

"Why's that?" Stitcher asked. His eyes perused the sheet music on the piano. "Is that because you'll disappear? I know you won't ever let me see your faces. If I turn around, you fade away like Eurydice. I'll bet you're not even as good looking as the Hydra. You don't scare me like you did when I was 14, you damn ghosts!"

The voice groaned. Or moaned. "We never mean to frighten you. We are not ghosts. Not quite. We are not damned either. Not yet. Remember that, Jacob Moses Gleaves."

Stitcher held back a shudder. He smiled. He waved his hand dismissively. "Just call me Stitcher, okay? If you keep calling me by my full name, we could be here all afternoon and cook bacon in the morning. Who are you anyway?"

"Emory Banks is how mortals knew me."

Stitcher smiled. "Oh yeah. Emory. I remember you. Too much fresh air mixed with your mustard gas. How's life treating you nowadays?"

"Your attempts at humor never quite coalesce."

Stitcher nodded. "Growing up a mortician's son leaves my comic shtick too deadpan." He smiled and pulled at his vest. "His turning the place into a gin joint when no funerals are going on helps a bit, though."

"Your father is a man of faith. He opened a tavern?"

"Business is slow since Black Friday." He shook his head. "Sure drained the swamp of greenbacks. What little of them that grew on trees down here in the bayou, anyhow. People are still dying, but fewer of them can afford to do it. Pops can keep the money flowing to help them get buried with respect. The white folks do okay for the most part, but some of the colored folks are like empty milk bottles; all 'poored' out. We're both God-fearing men doing God's work; that's all."

"Your father is part of what we came to talk about." Emory said, his voice drifting over the length of the bar like a calm brook. "The Skein is needed again."

Stitcher stood straight up to his six-foot-plus-height. "The Skein? Heck no! I buried him in the cemetery of the Great War! The Army had me pulling our dead boys out of the ditches for burial." Stitcher shrugged. "Guess they couldn't think of a better use for me since I grew up in a mortuary. I knew how to ride a horse carrying a corpse, that's all."

"A body snatcher stealing bodies from behind enemy lines for burial. That is quite a leap to counter-spy."

"I just did that on my time off for good behavior. Playing piano in the bars at night let me listen in to conversations. I overheard some by accident. I caught Kaiser's liars and sewed them into body bags with green thread. I told the M.P.s to look for the bags with green thread and got them out before they belonged there. I guess I've always been a bit quixotic that way. Those Kraut spies were too dumb to think a colored man could be smart. Joke's on them, though. After that, Army intelligence recruited me gave me a gas gun to field test."

"It was designed for shooting deadly gas," Emory reminded.

"It wasn't designed for anything. The field guys came up with the idea. At first, it shot out hot steam. That'll slow a soldier coming at you with a bayonet. 'Embalming gas' I came up with myself. It don't kill, but it keeps them on ice. The army can't question dead spies."

"The skills you have acquired will serve you well as The Skein."

"Skein's dead now, you understand? I buried him with you and all the rest of the stiffs back in the war! I started hearing all you dead-brains buzzing around after I saw that weird light in the sky. Lots of guys saw that light, but it affected each of us in different ways. I'm the only one that can talk to ya'll. First voice I heard said, 'The Skein'. That was it. Some kind of angel, I guess."

"About that…"

"Forget about that! I don't want to hear your caterpillar smoke again. I'm just glad you blasted ghosts stopped bugging me. I didn't miss you fellas constant yammerin' one bit or two bits. The Skein is dead. You can't bring him back!"

"You can bring him back anytime you are ready. You might have no choice now. It may be the only way to save your father. It may be the only way to save Lucille."

"My dad? My gal? They've nothing to do with it. Do they?"

"They do not have anything to do with it. They will."

"Don't be so cryptic, creep."

"Just be ready, Stitcher. You will know soon enough."

Stitcher turned to face the speaker. Only a slight whiff of smoke drifted there. The front door opened, allowing a breeze to carry it into oblivion. "Hey, Stitcher," Lucille's sweet voice said. He turned toward the door. Lucille shut it behind her. Lucille wore her sun dress. Looking at her was like looking at the sun. So beautiful it hurt his eyes.

He smiled. "Lucille, baby! What are you doing here?"

Lucille rushed to Stitcher. She threw her arms around his neck. She pressed her warm body against his and kissed his cheek. "I was just thinking about you!" Her face fell as she pulled away. "What's wrong, baby?"

Stitcher smiled broader. "Nothing now that you and your gorgeous gams are here, Lucille!" He drew her close for a deeper kiss. "Nothin' at all! Mardi Gras is coming up. We need to get the place ready!"

"Where is your dad?"

Stitcher waved his hand towards the door. "It's Sunday, baby. Dad always goes to Mass." He shrugged. "I can't go this week. I've got to clean up the joint. Can I meet you later?"

Lucille's lips parted, but stayed silent as the door creaked open again. Stitcher and Lucille looked to see Stitcher's father, Joseph Gleaves, standing there. Joe wore his best suit. Fit for church. Fit for a funeral. Joe pointed a revolver toward the floor. Joe pointed his eyes at nothing in particular. "Hello, Mister Gleaves," Lucille said.

Mr. Gleaves did not reply. His blank-check cornea watered. Stitcher whispered to Lucille, "Stay here baby." He walked toward his father. "Hey pops. What's up?"

Joseph Gleaves raised the pistol at his Lucille. Stitcher recoiled instinctively against Lucille to protect her. "Oh," she breathed.

A bullet whizzed past him, striking Lucille in the stomach. "No, dad!" Stitcher fell to his knees, cradling Lucille's bleeding body. "No! No! No!"

Stitcher growled as he stood to his feet, gently cradling Lucille as he lifted her with him. "Why, pops? Why?"

Aiming the pistol, Joe Gleaves croaked, "I'm sorry, son..." Stitcher heard the click of the hammer, then the deafening blast. He saw his blood stream through the air before passing out.

It was dark when Stitcher awoke. His head throbbed. He brought his hand to the drying blood caked to his hair. He grimaced as he felt the gash on his head, still warm from where the hot bullet burrowed over his scalp. He whispered a prayer of thanks that the bullet had not pierced his skull, and the wound seemed superficial.

He looked around in the gloom. He fished around in his pockets for a box of matches. From his still-seated position, he struck one against the floor. Flame burst forth, flashing over his cornea. He blinked his eyes until becoming used to the dim light. Holding his head, he stood up and went to the lantern on the top of the piano. Taking it by the handle, he placed the burning match to the wick. After adjusting the wick's length to send the light around copiously, he waved it around the room. The investigation displayed two pools of blood. One his, one Lucille's. Stitcher clenched his fists.

"Stitcher." The voice of Emory Banks. Barely audible.

Biting his lip, Stitcher growled, "I don't want to talk, Banks."

"Stitcher, Lucille is alive. You can yet rescue her."

"Why should I believe you? You're just a ghost!"

"When has a ghost lied to you?"

Stitcher nodded slowly. "A damn sight less often than living people, that's for sure. That's only as far as I know. I gotta get Lucille back, and settle things with pops."

"Capital," the ghost spoke in a wisp of air. "I have some suggestions. That is if you are willing to listen to reason."

Stitcher shut his eyes in pain and held his temple with his right hand. "Not doing anything more important than bleeding. Good thing it looks like I'm about done. Shoot the dice, spirit."

A bit louder than before; Emory Banks said, "Get out Skein."

"A stitch out of time? You're right." Stitcher's eyes glowered with the lantern's illumination. "The foxes have raided the chicken house, and The Skein is on the hunt."

Banks laughed. "Now you are talking, old chap!"

Stitcher walked to the basement door. He carried the lantern down the stairs in silence, the light illuminating the embalming tables and coffins of Gleaves Mortuary Service. He walked past shiny embalming instruments to a military chest resting against one wall. He pulled out a string from around his neck and dangled the skeleton key on its end. The key plunged into the padlock. With a turn, the device groaned and clicked open. Rust flakes dropped from to the ground as he removed the iron lock. Stitcher took a deep breath and threw the lid open. He put in his hand, returning it with a full-head gasmask.

"What did you expect to find, Stitcher? Did you think us 'ghosts' would fly out?"

"I wish you'd shut up, Emory, but I don't expect that. Why didn't they send a ghost that would shut the hell up?"

"I do not know of any. They call me the 'quiet one'."

"Yeah? Then shut up." Stitcher held turned the gasmask over-and-over in the dim light. It was made of black leather. Two round metal rings circled the dark glass viewports around the eyes. A red design of a pointed, cross-shaped dagger imitated a mouth. The tip of the 'blade' ended on the left side of the caricatured features. Stitcher put down the mask. He pulled out the Army pants, jacket, black leather boots, and wide-brimmed hat of a cavalry man.

Emory whistled. "Looks sharp, Stitcher."

Stitcher nodded. "Yep. I'm not wearing it, though. I've got fancier duds now."

"Yes," Emory said. "People might recognize those."

Stitcher nodded. "You've got a point there. I never wore my uniform as The Skein anyway. Gives something away about me, doesn't it?"

"It gives away that you were in the Army Cavalry. It would not take too much to guess you were in the 10th Cavalry, which would suggest your heritage."

"We don't want that," Stitcher replied. "People can guess, but that's all I want 'em doing. Guessing's better than wholesale lynchings like happened in Florida."

"So what will you wear?"

"What every dead man wears-a suit and tie." Stitcher laughed sardonically. "Dressed to the nines for my own funeral. That'll save time, now won't it?"

"Perhaps. Still, your uniform is more durable. You have not worn it in over a decade. No one would recognize you if you remove the medals and bars."

Taking off his shirt, Stitcher took out the Army issue one and put it on. "Hey, it still fits! I take it out and wash it every year, just for old times sake." He removed his pants and shoes, replacing them with the Army pants and boots. Soon, he wore the complete uniform, minus decorations and honors. He donned the cavalry hat last. He walked over to the large mirror in the corner to look at the result. He patted his chest. "Still looks good after all this time."

"You were only 17-years-old when the war ended."

"Do you never stop talking, Emory? If you make an opening in your neck, the mustard gas can get out there instead of whistling between your teeth."

"You can forget the levity. It needs pressing. I can help."

Stitcher gritted his teeth. "You're right. I need to get going." Reaching into the chest once more, he retrieved his 0.45 revolver in its holder and strapped it over his shoulder, leaving the pistol hanging over his left hip. He lifted the Embalmizer and its specially-designed holster. The modified Colt 0.45 automatic had a thick, cylindrical handle. He tested the handle by opening it and placing one of the metallic gas cartridges into it. He removed the cartridge and put the Embalmizer in his jacket pocket. He looked at the cylindrical gas cartridges he held in his hand. "I need to make fresher stuff."

"Where will you get what you need to make it?"

Stitcher waved his arms around the room. "Right here, of course. I just mixed up some arsenic embalming fluid with some other preservative chemicals. Pops went to college to learn this stuff. He taught me how to use it real young."

Though Emory did not reply, Stitcher still felt the ghostly presence. Walking to the workbench, Stitcher retrieved vials of powder and chemical from the shelves. He shook his head as he dumped powder from the cylinders. Placing the gasmask over his face he began mixing chemicals in vials. He used the long metal embalming needles to collect the resulting liquid, which he then drained into the metal gas cylinders.

"How do you make the gas?"

Stitcher shook his head. "You saw me do it."

"Our minds do not retain minutia."

Stitcher laughed as he placed the vials into the breast pocket of his jacket. "Nice to know I can have some secrets from you!"

"I am glad that you are pleased."

"To no end, pal. To no end." Stitcher looked over his uniform. He took some black riding gloves off a shelf and put them on. He placed his cavalry hat snuggly over his gasmask and returned to the mirror for a final look. "How do I look, Emory?"

Emory laughed lowly. "Like death, Stitcher."

Stitcher nodded grimly. "Someone messed with my loved ones. I'm gonna look like death to someone."

Stitcher walked up the steps leading outside of the cellar.

"You do not mind if I accompany you, I hope."

Stitcher sneered as he turned around. The moon outlined his strange form. Emory showed himself as a stream of swamp gas that rose into the cool night air. Stitcher dissipated it with a sweep of his gloved hand. "There's your answer, Union Jack."

Stitcher turned to look at the graves. The cemetery stood fifty yards behind Joe Gleaves Place. Swamp gasses escaped the stone crypts. Mists rose from the headstones. He walked toward the mortuary's garage. He opened the wooden doors and walked past the horse-drawn but now horseless hearse. Heading toward a stable behind it, he walked up to the Andalusian waiting inside. Stitcher smiled as he patted the horse on snout. "Hey there, Lazarus. How are things? Ready for a ride?"

The horse snorted.

Stitcher laughed. "Good! It's gonna be a long night."

Stitcher retrieved the tack and saddle and went to the task of preparing Lazarus.

A bad feeling came over Officer Alvin Harbow, but it didn't overcome him. Grasping the steering wheel of the Desoto, he turned to his partner. "Damn, Tom-doesn't this time of year give you the creeps?"

Thomas Barrett pushed his hat back and nodded. "If I thought about it too much, every day in this town would give me shivers. Creepy little town you got here."

Al sighed. "Maybe we could call it a night?"

Tom shook his head. "We took the graveyard shift. If we go in early, we won't get paid extra."

"Not sure it's worth it, Tom. Not in this town."

"You do know how much we're getting paid to be out here."

"Sure, it's good money. That's a not always worth it."

"Look Al. I know this town's like reading a book by Stoker, but nothing hardly happens here."

"Who's Stoker?"

"Who's Stoker? Don't you read?"

"Sure I do. Police reports. Every day. That's plenty wild for me. So, who's Stoker?"

"He wrote Dracula."

"What's that?"

"It's about some rich, punk hood that goes around sucking blood out of poor folk."

"Was this Stoker guy a Russian or something?"

Tom rolled his eyes. "Forget it. We've got another five hours on this shift. I'll shut my eyes for a nickel of time. Wake me up, and then you can sleep."

Harbow peered through the night gloom. "I wish they'd get some streetlights out here."

"It's too close to the bayou. Can't put a lamp here in nowhere. You gonna let me catch a wink or what?"

"Sorry, Barrett." Harbow stared into the bayou's darkness as Tom slept. Shadows moved about. Indistinct. Undefined. His eyes and his mind played tricks on him. He wiped his brow, thinking he saw a glowing ignis fatuus rise out of the swamp. He bit his tongue to remain silent. The will-o-wisp faded as he continued watching it. He continued looking at the marsh. He thought of waking Officer Barrett, but did not.

The glowing ignis fatuus orb reappeared. Clearly visible, it moved toward the car at a slow, steady pace. "Tom!" he shouted. "A will-o-wisp!"

Rubbing his eyes, Tom Barrett sat up. He stared with his partner. "It sure is, Al!"

"What should we do?"

They peered through the darkness as the orb approached. The moonlight outlined a shaped behind the glowing orb. "It's not an will-o-wisp! Someone's carrying a lantern through the marsh!"

Al's brow furrowed. "At this time of night?"

Tom shrugged. "Best to carry a lantern at night, I guess. Carrying one in daylight doesn't do much good."

Al bit his lip. "We should check it out! Nobody's up this late unless it's to cause trouble."

"Why are we up, then?" Nodding, Tom took his revolver out of the holster. He looked at Al who did the same. They nodded to each other and opened their doors.

The figure carrying the lantern came closer and closer. "Hey you!" Barrett shouted. "Come over here!"

The figure silently obeyed without quickening its pace or changing direction. Illuminated by the lantern it carried, its features began to show as it approached. A tall, stout figure came slowly into view. He wore an ankle-length long coat of many colors, all of them faded; green, grey, blue, brown, red, orange, yellow, sallow. His nose appeared as an absurdly elongated beak, yet his smooth, caramel-skinned face seemed real. He wore a wide-brimmed, flat-topped hat over his bald head. His outfit recalled the word 'plague' to the mind of Officer Barrett. The word 'shambling' best described his gait.

Officers Barrett and Harbow backed away. Tom smiled. "You're a big one, aincha? Got your costume out a bit early, doncha think?"

Silent aside from the shambling sounds he made, the figure kept coming. Al's eyes widened. "He's making me nervous!"

Tom Barrett took on a more defensive stance as the figure kept coming. "You can stop right there! We just want to ask you a few questions."

Not offering a reply, nor indicating he'd even heard Tom, the figure retained its forward motion toward the car. Al backed away. "He's not gonna stop!"

"What can he do?" Tom asked. "The car's in his way!"

Not really wanting an answer, the officers received one. The hulking man loomed over the car. His enormous shadow fell across the windshield. He tipped the lantern over the hood. A handful of Mardi Gras beads sparked as they rolled onto the car. The gold, purple, and green spheres rolled around, releasing a haze of smoke.

Tom and Al coughed as they breathed in the smoke. Brandishing his revolver, Al ran after the uncanny figure. "Get away from the car!"

Tom aimed his gun at the large man as he opened the car door on his side. "You heard my partner, pal! Back off!"

The massive man continued his impression of a slow moving freight train.

"Get in!" Al shouted as he slid behind the steering wheel. Tom hopped into the car. Al put the car in reverse.

"What," Tom said, "are we gonna run from a guy taking a late night walk?"

Al nodded vehemently. "Hell yes! Did you see that crusher?" The man began moving faster.

Tom shrugged. "I don't know if it means we should run away!"

"It's a good start! I'm not gonna shoot a guy for walking toward our car!" Al spun the car around as the lantern-carrying behemoth quickened his pace. Al floored the accelerator.

Tom looked behind them. "He's speeding up!"

Al gritted his teeth. "He can't keep up with a V-8!"

Tom shook his head. "Looks like he might!"

"What?" Al turned the corner, almost tipping the car on its side. "Nobody's that fast!"

"I wish it would hold true!" Tom said. "It doesn't look like it much! What's he gonna do if he catches up?"

"I don't plan to find out!" Al said. "I'm not a coward, but I'm not taking chances over nothing!"

Tom watched as the man seemed to keep pace with the sedan. "If he's dangerous, it's our duty to stop him!"

"When he does something to something or someone, we'll deal with that then! Right now, I'm protecting his life and ours!"

In front of the squad car, Skein appeared on horseback. The rider headed toward the car. "What the heck is that? It's gonna hit us!"

Al tried to swerve the car to miss the rider on horseback. The horse and rider remained stock-still. Tom put his arms over his face and screamed as the car threatened collision with the horse and rider.

Stitcher rode Lazarus slowly next to the car. "What are you officers doing?" he asked in a deep tone.

Tom opened his eyes and looked about. He rolled down the window. "Who are you?"

"I am The Skein." He shook his head. "No time to explain. I am on your side, if you are on mine. What are you doing?"

Tom and Al looked out the back window. Al cleared his throat. "We're getting away from that guy chasing us!"

"Yeah!" Tom agreed.

Stitcher looked down the road. "I see no one."

"He's not there now, but he was!" Al looked to make sure of his statement. "A huge cuss, too! We thought he was a wisp at first. He came out of the swamp and chased our squad car!"

The Skein looked over the vehicle. "Your car isn't running."

Al looked around. "Hey, Tom-we haven't moved!"

The Skein nodded as he got down from Lazarus. "You gentlemen have been hypnotized." He put his gloved hand on their hood. "Your engine is cold. Tell me all that occurred."

Tom related the events up until they tried to get away from the man. Stitcher stopped him when he started the chase. "The gas made you susceptible to hypnotic suggestion. I doubt this man was as big as he appeared to you, or had the long nose."

Tom shrugged. "But we saw him before he dropped the marbles, or was even close to us!"

"You were watching his lantern as he walked toward the car." The Skein suggested. "It is classic Mesmerism suggestion. The specifics of how he did it are wanting."

Al scratched his head. "I guess that might be it. It's still a bit much to take."

"I have seen this kind of gypsy parlor trick before," The Skein assured. "Simple stage magic with some drugs mixed in." Stitcher bent over and

*He put his gloved hand on their hood. "Your engine is cold."*

picked up a green bead and rolled it around between his gloved fingers. "Can I take this?"

Al shrugged. "Sure. Take as many as you want."

"One will do," Stitcher assured as he dropped it into his breast pocket. "I suggest you do not report any of this event, including about me."

"Wait a minute, pal," Officer Harbow said. "What are you doing in the get up? I see you're packing heat too. Maybe you need to come in for questioning."

Stitcher peered through the round holes in his mask. "I think we could keep this friendly, officer. If you bring me in, I might have to bring up the story you just told me."

"Hey!" Tom protested. "That really happened!"

"I believe you," Stitcher said. "Your fellow officers might not be so understanding."

"Yeah, but…" Tom continued, "You could be in cahoots with that hoodoo guru man!"

Al shook his head. "Forget it, Tom. He's right. He hasn't broken any serious law to bring him in. We can just leave this friendly-for now." Officer Harbow looked right at The Skein. "Okay, SKEIN, you stay on the right side of the law."

The Skein remounted his horse. "You might help me as well. I am looking for some people. They were kidnapped earlier tonight. Your swamp magician is likely involved."

Tom nodded. "If someone's it trouble, we've got to help. Do you think the swamp guy kidnapped these people?"

"I do not." The moonlight glinted off of the eye-ports. "There is something larger going on. The swamp trickster is part of it. You were attacked for a reason. The kidnappings happened the same day. It is not a coincidence. I'm certain of that. Just stay alert, and try to solve the kidnapping case."

The Skein goaded Lazarus forward, taking off at a gallop.

Tom turned to his partner. "What now, Al?"

Al sighed. "I'm for calling it a night."

"Our shift's not over yet. Maybe we can look through the police files."

Al got into the driver's seat and started the engine. "Sounds like a better way to spend our time."

Tom smiled as he got in. The sedan disappeared into the misty night.

❦ ❦ ❦

A lone rider in Stygian darkness, The Skein made his way through the treacherous bayou. The moon cast long shadows of trees and the strange rider. The mist and tall grass danced together in surreal waves, bending Luna's light through a jittery path.

Stitcher's eyes moved through the glade. Watching every movement of nocturnal beast or waving branch, his keen senses allowed a deceivingly-easy path through the limpid pools of mud-and-vegetation choked water.

Lazarus let out a nervous whinny. The Skein patted the horse on its neck. As he surveyed his surroundings, he began to see patterns of recent movement through the tall grass. He discovered where the swamp magician walked, breaking off and trampling plants as he traveled. The Skein nodded at the discovery.

A patch of cloud obscured the moon, leaving The Skein at a disadvantage. He listened acutely to pick out the path while his eyes adjusted to the dim light. He entered a grove of trees and stopped. A quiet rustling noise started some several yards away. He raised his head to listen. The noise grew increasingly louder. Stitcher dismounted from Lazarus and pulled his gas-gun.

"Come out!" Stitcher shouted in challenge. He searched the impenetrable darkness of the grove. "I'm on solid ground! Show yourselves!"

The rustling ceased. Stitcher breathed in deeply. A group of some twenty people broke forth from the trees. Dirty and disheveled men, women, and children appeared from behind the trees and climbed through the tall swamp-grass. Despite their varied skin-tones indicating descent from all continents, the shared the distinction of being from the human race.

They shuffled slowly toward The Skein, moonlight glinting off their clouded, soulless eyes. They howled and slavered before rushing forward, holding their arms straight in front of them to grasp at The Skein's strange figure. He released a stream of the yellow embalming gas from his weirdly-engineered pistol as the crowd reached him.

The effects of the gas displayed on a man and two women rushing for Stitcher. They fell to the ground, their teeth gnashing in spasms with their uncontrollably twitching bodies.

Stitcher quickly looked behind before retreating. He reloaded a gas cartridge into the Embalmizer. A second wave stumbled over the three on the ground in a gone-amok attempt to reach Skein.

The first three struck by the gas stood again to their feet and headed at The Skein. Stitcher released another stream of the gas as the grouping of seven ravenous creatures approached him. The creatures were no longer human. Stitcher refused to think it, but the word came to him. It seeped through his subconscious and verbalized inaudibly in his mind. A ghostly voice from behind him whispered, Zombies.

The Skein shook his head. "Shufflers," he said. The four newly-joining Shufflers fell to the ground when the gas struck. The first three he'd fired at continued, unhampered this time by the gas. Skein pulled his revolver and fired at the man among them. The bullet struck the zombie in the chest. Embalming gas streamed from his mouth and nostrils.

One woman came forward, the other stumbling over the new obstacle of the dead zombie and falling to the ground. Skein gritted his teeth and used his boot to kick her into one of the fetid ponds.

"That's cold, son!" Stitcher heard from behind him.

"Shut up, Emory! I'm working here!"

"You think I'm Emory?" the voice asked as the other zombie woman stood to her feet. A line formed behind her to get their chance at Skein. "I'm not that stiff-necked beanpole! I'm hurt, Stitcher. Don't you remember me? It's Jonathan Afton!"

Stitcher put in another cartridge. "Johnny? Why do you guys bug me when I'm busy?"

"You're always busy, Stitcher. We're here to help. What do you think will happen when these zombies go loose on Mardi Gras?"

The four felled by the last blast of gas rose to join the others. Stitcher fired the Embalmizer again, felling another wave of joiners. "They ain't gonna be here for the festivities, if I have my way. If you're here to help, let me do my damn job!"

"How's that gonna help, Stitch?"

Stitcher laughed as he pocketed his Embalmizer and drew his revolver. "I'd rather shoot you than these zombies just to get you to shut the hell up! But you're dead, and these dead things ain't gonna let me alone!" He fired the pistol.

"Are you sure they're dead, Stitch?"

The Skein looked at the zombie he shot as it fell. Blood pumped from the wound. "They're not dead!"

"Thought it might make a difference to you," Johnny said.

"The gas won't work, but bullets will kill 'em!"

Johnny laughed. "That's what guns do. What're you gonna do?"

"The best I can." Pulling right leg in the air, Skein kicked a male zombie on its chin.

"Using your feet, Stitch," Johnny said, "That's using your head! Did you learn that move playing football?"

Stitcher shrugged. "Thought you specters knew everything." Skein spun around, delivering a kick to a zombie's chest. "My dad taught me boxing and French Savate as a kid. He wanted me to be able to fight, in case those sheet-ghosts came to burn a cross."

"When'd you have time to learn all the stuff you know?"

"The War. Buryin' you stiffs didn't take all day." Skein punched another zombie. "Made money for college racin' bikes on the Motordromes. Came home to help pa and get a girl."

"You got a girl," Johnny said. "Lucille."

"If she's still alive." The zombies rushed. Skein smiled grimly beneath the gasmask. He toppled the lead zombie with a kick to her midriff. "This could take all night!"

Johnny chuckled. "If you can keep it up all night, Stitch."

Stitcher nodded. "You know damn well that's not the only option. It's also not the best one." Stitcher let out a piercing whistle. "Lazarus!" he shouted.

The horse galloped forward, knocking over zombies as he came to The Skein's command. Kicking a zombie away, Stitcher leapt into the saddle. "We'll get this done later!"

Skein watched as zombies streamed out of the grove. They rushed Lazarus and pushed the horse over through the power of sheer weight. Lazarus released a terrified whinny as the zombies began biting the horse with their teeth.

Stitcher drew his revolver. Zombies grabbed at him as he rolled away and leapt to his feet. He fired at the zombies attacking Lazarus, striking their arms and legs with minimal effect. Zombies surrounded him as he took aim.

"Get up, Lazarus!" Stitcher shouted. "Come on!"

Despite the teeth biting into him, Lazarus rose to his feet. He bucked, knocking away several of the zombies. The Skein punched at one of the zombies. "That's it, boy! Come get me!"

The horse became a fury. His bucking sent his attackers flying through the air. Retrieving the Embalmizer, Skein released a stream of gas on the zombies. This knocked down several. Others came toward him over the fallen zombies. Lazarus galloped through them, knocking them to the ground.

Skein grasped the reins of the fast-moving horse and swung himself into the saddle in one quick motion. He patted Lazarus on the neck. "Good boy! Let's head home. We need to change plans."

Lazarus remained a bit shaken from the ordeal. The horse moved quickly through the swamp as Stitcher stole a glance behind them. Without a target, the zombies wandered into darkness.

❦ ❦ ❦

Sore. That word popped into Stitcher's head when he awoke and all through breakfast. He remained sore while walking to the barn. He went out to check on Lazarus. "Hey Lazarus!"

The horse stood up in the stall and trotted to Stitcher. "Hey, old boy," Stitcher said. He patted the horse's head. He looked over the teeth marks on the horse. "I looked at these last night, but let's give you a better going over today." He pulled at the horse's hair. "It doesn't look like they punctured your skin. I'd hate to bite through horsehide too! Here's an eyetooth stuck in your side."

Stitcher pulled a piece of sugar from his pocket and gave it to the horse. Lazarus picked it up with his lips. Stitcher ran his hand over the horse's mane. "I'm not taking you with me this time, Lazarus. I needed you last night. Two brains are better than one in the swamp." He sighed. "I saw those swamp shufflers really got to you, so I'm taking the bike today. I've got a lot of ground to cover. You just rest up."

Lazarus let out a whinny as Stitcher walked across the garage. "It'll be okay," Stitcher said. He pulled a tarp off of a green motorcycle. He silently read the word Excelsior on its gas tank.

"I can use this bike just fine."

"Didn't you have to pull bodies out of the trenches with this?" A hollow voice said from behind.

Stitcher clenched his teeth. "Who's this?"

"Dang, Stitch." The ghostly voice said. "Doncha remember yer old pal? It's Harlem Charlie!"

Stitcher blinked. "Charlie? Dammit, why'd you have to come!"

"Man Stitch," Charlie's ghost said, "I thought we was pals!"

Stitcher resisted the urge to turn around. "Pals! You were like a brother to me! It killed me to sew you into your sugar-sack!"

"I know, Stitcher. That's why it had to be me, brother!"

"Why? So you damn ghosts could torment me some more?"

"You think you're gonna get the face behind these zombies? The gas don't work on 'em. You know that."

"I figured that out already. Gas don't work when they don't breathe much. Their lungs don't get enough." Stitcher shrugged. "I can still take this punk down."

"Man, you're a thick one aincha? Ain't gonna be that easy. This's no punk, I'll tell ya that for free! What in the hell do you think this is all about, Stitcher?"

"You tell me!"

"Okay," the ghost whispered in zephyr-like tones. "Just hear this. You never had trouble listenin', but you couldn't hear."

Stitcher breathed in deep. "I'm hearing. Let's hear it."

Harlem Charlie's voice fell gently on Stitcher's ear. "Okay, Stitcher. You left the Army with full honors. That was more than a decade ago. You followin'?"

Stitcher nodded. "I'm following like a spider follows the web-strand to the fly. Go on. After that I worked my way through college racing bikes in the Motodrome. Cut the biography."

"Don't go off in a huff! Do you suppose your pop shot you for fun? What it's all about, Stitch, is you."

"What? Why?"

"Well, you can talk to us ghosts, right?"

"Only when ya'll want."

"Sure, sure. It ain't a matter of wantin' anyhow, but you got it. Didn't you guess The Skein would be a threat to someone?"

"After all this time?"

"Yep. 'After 'all this time'."

"Nobody knows I'm The Skein! Hell, I don't know that anybody even knows about Skein!"

"Yeeessss," Charlie drew the word into a hiss. "We do."

Stitcher kicked the motorcycle. "Damn it! I thought you fellas would only talk to me!"

"We do," Harlem Charlie assured. "Don't you think someone might know that you talk to us? Mebbe they saw the telephone wires buzzin'."

"Don't give me 'maybe' Charlie. I didn't even tell my girl or my father about the 'dead letter office' where you guys sent your confessions. I need to know how. I need to know who!"

"Heck, Stitcher. That ain't the way it works."

Stitcher got on the motorcycle. "Tell me what you can."

"I can't tell you no more, Stitcher." Charlie's voice quavered. "You know we're still pals, doncha?"

"I told you before," Stitcher said, "We're brothers. Except I'm feeling like Cain right now, and I'm thinking about finding a big rock to plow into your head."

"I can tell you where to find the answers."

"Then whisper away."

"On the abandoned Smelt Plantation."

Stitcher pulled the gasmask over his face and placed an army helmet over it. "Thanks, brother. I'm going now."

The engine drowned Charlie's whisper as the motorcycle roared to life. "Take care, Charlie!" Stitcher drove the motorcycle through the garage doors and into the swamp.

"This damnable road," Harbow said.

Tom nodded. "'Damnable' is right. Where the hell we going?"

"Where the picture with that clown from the other night says," Al said as he held a child's drawing of the large, strangely-dressed figure into the air. The words "the plantation" and "1812" were scrawled across the bottom. "You're the one who found it buried in the file cabinets. To 'the plantation'."

"It doesn't say what plantation. There must be hundreds of them around Louisiana!"

"There must be," Officer Harbow agreed. "So we play Sheerluck Homes. There weren't as many plantations around here in 1812. There's fewer near the river that old. We'll try the abandoned ones. I think the burnt-out Smelt place is a good one to start."

The car jostled down the road. Tom placed his hand against the ceiling to keep from hitting it. They saw a wall of shufflers blocking the road, moving slowly toward them.

"What's that?" Tom asked.

"I don't know," Al said, stopping the car. "They don't look right to me. They all look sick!"

Tom pulled his hat down. "Leave the engine running and stay in the car. I'll handle this."

He opened got out and faced the crowd. "Stop! Tell me what's going on here."

The crowd stared through Barrett. "I said halt!"

Unheeding, they flowed past him as a river does a tree. Tom pulled his pistol. "Stop, damn you! I'm an officer of the law!"

The words fell on dead ears. Tom moved grabbed a deathly-pale woman. "Where're you going?"

The woman's face twisted into a snarl as she used her long fingernails to claw at him. Tom released her as the others shufflers took notice.

She rushed Tom, her hair waving, pulled by current from the imaginary river. He rushed toward the car, plunging through the crowd. The people surrounded him and began punching, scratching, clawing, and gnashing. Moving away again, he brandished his gun. "First come, first serve!"

Unheeding, they shuffled toward him. He let a punch fly against a portly man. Stunned, the man fell back. He kicked at another, a teenage boy, knocking him to the ground. They struggled upright again. He saw no clear exit. The odds of thirty-to-one seemed insurmountable, though Tom rushed into the fray. "Harbow!" he yelled. "A hand here?"

Tom leapt aside as the squad car struck the shufflers.

"Get in!" shouted Officer Harbow as he flung the door open.

Tom rushed to the door and jumped in. "What the heck's going on here, Al?"

"I don't know," Harbow admitted. Gunning the car in reverse. "Let's figure it out."

"You hit those people with the car!" Tom shouted as he pulled the door shut. "Is that how police handle things here?"

"I saved your soft, Yankee skin!" Harbow said. "They were gonna rip you to shreds! Some gratitude."

Skein rode his motorcycle through the swamp, carefully choosing a familiar path. He rode over rickety, makeshift bridges placed haphazardly over pools of slimy water or murky streams. Tall plants tugged at his boots, impairing the motorcycle's progress along the weed-choked paths and unused roads. Stitcher knew where he headed. Familiar odors crept toward the sky. Familiar animals scampered into the brush. They dove into holes, slithered into clumps of grass, and climbed trees. The machine stole from the denizens of the swamp their lazy, death-a-minute repose they felt in the familiarity of the fetid swamp.

Stitcher felt at home here, in the bayou; a child's playground of deadly gators, cats, and serpents. Burying things proved as impermanent as the bayou. Here, there was no such thing as lifeless rot. The swamp-ooze filled with dead leaves, grass, and branches incubated and housed the creatures. Here, death encouraged life.

Stitcher abandoned these notions as he spied his objective. Crawling vines smothered the pale mansion. Vines, the bane of an abandoned plantation, grew feet in a day. Stitcher rode over the vines that moved as a stream of torpid snakes. Stitcher could feel them roll under the motorcycle, though they lay still. The bike tires moved them. They did not grow as fast as imagined. He rolled the machine through the mansion's sagging iron gates. Hinges rusted through. Their blood spilled in rusted flakes to the ground. Vines, here too, worked to attack the gates of hell.

Stitcher stopped the motorcycle inside the courtyard. Threatening suicide, the mansion leaned toward the Mississippi river some one hundred yards away, barely visible through the thick, vine-draped trees and brush. Trees lined the courtyard; young trees, old trees, ancient trees. It created an example of eternal twilight. The sun seeped through, finding every free course available.

Stitcher breathed in the air, full of stench even through the filter of his gasmask. He slowly rode toward the mansion.

As he approached, a figure appeared in the dilapidated doorway. Darkness surrounded the man; tall, with an impossibly hooked nose, and wearing a long Joseph's coat of many colors. Stitcher stopped the motorcycle and turned off the engine.

"See?" Charlie's voice. Stitcher smelled the ghost's breath, swamp gas and onion. "I told you this is where you'll find answers." The Skein got off his motorcycle, leaning it against a tree.

Stitcher waved the ghost away. He looked at the figure in the door. "Drop the façade. I know it's an illusion."

The behemoth of a man shifted to his right, his nose swaying as he did so. "You think this is not my face? That this is a mask? Yet, this resembles a face. Your face is the horrific one!"

"Horrific?" The Skein replied. "Good. Be terrified."

The figure laughed. "I am the Prince of all that is horrid Mister Gleaves. I am Prêtre Ague."

Skein nodded. "The Plague Priest? I've heard them speak of you in France. You have quite a flare for melodrama. Priest is a title of respect. You have none. I will call you 'Mister Ague'."

Ague smiled broadly. "Call me what you wish, Mister Gleaves. You have not long to call anyone anything anymore."

While Ague spoke, shufflers filtered out of the stygian alcoves onto the porch. They stood dumbly next to Ague. They stared blankly at Skein. "You see, Mister Gleaves, my shufflers as you call them, are going to join the crowds during Mardi Gras by riverboat, yet you will not be there!" Mister Ague flourished his hand. "Kill him!" he shouted.

"You've got your shufflers out?" Skein pulled his .45 revolver as the shufflers shambled slowly toward him. "I know you are using zombie palm to control their souls."

Mister Ague shrugged as his minions drew near to Skein. "The knowledge avails you not in this, your final hour. The Zombia antillarium plant is, indeed, one part of the formula giving me control over the living as the undead. Your beliefs won't let you kill my zombies indiscriminately."

"Zombies? Slaves is more like it, and you're their master. Nothing's more repulsive to free men. My grandfather fought for his freedom, as did many men black and white, for freedom of all Americans." Skein fired at the nearest shuffler's knee, dropping it to the ground. "I don't have to kill them. I only have to remove their master."

He looked past the approaching shufflers to the porch. Ague turned from Skein's piercing gaze. "Cut off the head of Eden's snake, and the tail can't sting!"

Ague's pace quickened toward the black portal. "Abandon all hope, ye who enter here!" he shouted, disappearing into the gloomy interior.

"I'm going for a touchdown." Skein pushed the shufflers aside as he rushed past. He dodged their grasps with ease.

Skein heard a whispered voice behind him as he stared into darkened maw. "'Abandon all hope' is what he said, Stitcher. Outside, you can play football with these shufflers all day. Inside, you'll be caught in hell."

"I don't know who you are," Stitcher said, "but I 'abandoned all hope' a long time ago. I've a feeling Ague wants all hope gone, but I'm making my own batch!"

Skein caught glimpses of shufflers moving through mildewed doorways as he rushed in. He fired a stream from the Embalmerizer at the closest three. The changes he made to the gas seemed effective. They crumpled to the ground in the fumes.

Skein turned around to see a shuffler across the large, open room. The shuffler threw something toward him. The thick, finned, oblong, and dart-shaped projectile flew through the air.

"A Ketchum grenade!" Stitcher rushed forward, catching the black object like a football, and threw it back.

A whispered voice laughed behind Skein as the grenade headed toward its original thrower. "That could be bad, Stitcher."

Skein dove to the floor. The grenade exploded with a raucous sound. The blast sent splinters of rotten wood and debris through the air. Skein tried to stand to his feet, but could not. The floor groaned before collapsing. The floor buckled under him, sending him plummeting to an unknown depth.

Skein plunged into a steamy, swampy pool beneath the house. The splintered wood from the rotted floor hailed down in a barrage of deadly spears. Rubble from dependent walls and furnishings splashed in the stygian gloom around him.

Bits of the rubble plinked and pinged off his helmet. Skein held his head, his ears ringing from the blast. He stood up in the muck-filled bottom of the shallow pool.

Looking up, Stitcher saw immobile shufflers staring down at him from the remains of the destroyed floor. The sunlight lit the room above more copiously than before. Skein surmised a part of an outer wall had collapsed as well as the floor.

Ignoring the dead stares, Skein focused on the sound of splashing in the distance. He looked at the Embalmizer. He'd held the weapon tightly during the explosion. He breathed in deeply and moved toward the pool's sandy shore.

"Sounds like the 'gators are hungry, Stitcher."

"Shut up," Stitcher replied to the ethereal voice.

"Maybe I can help."

Stitcher nodded. "I never doubted you could. I just don't trust you would."

"That hurts, Stitcher."

"Good. My momma, God rest her soul, said I shouldn't hold conference with the dead anyway."

"So why do you do it?"

"Because you all won't shut the hell up, and I haven't figured out a way to make you."

"Let me show you that you can trust me," the spirit said. "Jump to your right, RIGHT NOW!"

Skein tensed his muscles and leapt away as an alligator took a snapping lunge at him out of the water. Stitcher grabbed the reptile around the throat as it passed through the air. He pulled it to the ground and held it as it writhed under his powerful grip.

"I guess you owe me an apology," the ghost said.

"Put it on my bar tab, punk." Skein dug in his jacket pocket with his left hand, still holding the deadly animal to the ground. He retrieved his revolver, holding the muzzle to the back of the alligator's head. The bullet made a loud bang as blood sprayed the area. Stitcher let the creature fall to the ground.

"Man, Stitcher," the voice said, "did you have to kill it?"

"Who do you think you're kidding? It didn't have to kill me, but if it had

*Looking up, Stitcher saw immobile shufflers staring down at him from the remains of the destroyed floor.*

a revolver to my head it would have done the same. It's just a 'gator. If you grew up around here, you wouldn't have any soft place for the damned animals."

"Who's the 'damned animal' here?"

"Shut the hell up."

"I can tell you how to get out of this rumrunner's cave."

"Tell me, or I swear I'll find a way to make you suffer."

The voice offered a sigh. "Follow the shoreline to your right. You'll see the light soon enough."

"Okay." Skein moved in the suggested direction.

"What?" the voice whispered. "No thanks for me?"

"Right. No thanks."

As Stitcher came around a large rock, he saw sunlight streaming through to the mouth of the cave some thirty yards distant. He soon stood on the shore of the mighty Mississippi River.

His eyes adjusted to the sunlight to see a dilapidated riverboat moored nearby. Vines hung off its sides, dangling in the water. The gangplank rested invitingly against the sandy shore. Skein moved back into the cave entrance as he saw a row of shufflers appear out of a grove of trees on the beach and ramble toward the boat. They shambled up the plank and into the craft.

With great caution, Stitcher moved up the shore and returned to the swamp. The shufflers took no notice. Once in the cover of the grass, he could see the path the shufflers used. He followed it back to the mansion. He saw no movement in the structure as he went to retrieve his motorcycle. It rested against the tree where he'd left it. It had not been moved or touched. Straddling the motorcycle, he kicked the pedals to start it up. The machine roared to life. He drove it toward the steamboat.

As he returned, he saw the riverboat pull away from shore. Cursing to himself, he rode quickly upriver to pursue. Approaching the boat, which quickly separated itself from the shore, he looked over at the shufflers lined up along its pair of encircling decks. Stitcher's heart jumped as he caught sight of Lucille. She stood over the enormous, spinning red paddle wheel. Skein gunned the throttle on his bike, spitting sand behind him. He rode recklessly down the shoreline, deftly avoiding tree branches overhanging the water. He slid into the water when necessary, the motorcycle spitting the muddy bottom high into the air.

He saw a dock on the river's bend ahead. He pushed the throttle to its limits. Skein ignored the engine's protests. He concentrated on reaching the wooden planks of the decaying dock. Reaching it, he slowed down only enough to plan a straight line down the dock, then returned the motorcycle to its highest speed.

Some twenty yards away, the steamboat slowed as it rounded the bend. As Skein reached the end of the dock, he pulled the handlebars back to lift the front wheel. It landed atop of one of the jutting pilings. The rear wheel struck the makeshift piling, creating a puff of smoke as the motorcycle launched and went flying over the water and through the air.

Making a split-second decision, Skein calculated the distance to the boat and the motorcycle's descent. He stood up on the gas tank. Using his powerful leg muscles to propel him forward, he leapt from the machine. The motorcycle crashed into the riverboat's railing, becoming entangled in the bent metal. Skein leapt away from the impact, his boot striking the railing. He toppled onto the deck, rolling as if he carried a football.

Shufflers on the deck moved toward him. Stitcher struggled to his feet as he freed his Embalmizer. He fired at the group of five shufflers approaching him. The shufflers quickened their pace. He drew his revolver, but did not need it. The shufflers fell into a coughing fit and tumbled to the deck.

The disembodied voice returned. "How'd you get that smoke trick of yours to work?"

Skein shook his head. "They don't breathe very often and their hearts beat slowly," he replied, "so I added a stimulant to the formula. It get them sucking in the gas, which knocks them out."

Three shufflers moved toward Skein as he released another stream of smoke from his gun. The shufflers folded to the deck. A female shuffler staggered to the railing, bent awkwardly over it before plunging into the water. Stitcher holstered the Embalmizer and rushed to the railing. A large shuffler grabbed him as he climbed over.

"Let me go!" Stitcher said, as he struggled. "She'll drown!"

Ague appeared, brandishing a pistol. "Yes. She will drown."

"Let me save her, you blasted savage!" Skein snarled.

Ague yawned. "If you can, you may."

Skein cast his captor over his shoulder and into Ague, sending the shuffler and the master violently to the wooden deck. Stitcher leapt over the railing, splashing into the murky water.

"Blast it!" Ague shouted as he rushed to the railing and fired into the swirling, enigmatic water. He watched the river, looking for a sign of Skein. "A boat full of minions and it is left to me to kill him!"

Skein searched the turgid river in vain for the fallen shuffler. His lungs threatened to burst as the helmet's weight threatened to foerce him down.

The mighty river pulled at him as he surfaced for air. A hail of bullets pocked the water with small, deadly splashes.

Skein dove below the river again. He stroked hard to swim under the water. Only a short glimpse of the shore in his brief excursion above the surface guided him.

"Stop the boat!" Ague ordered. "Get to the bank!"

Water churned under the paddles as the boat turned.

Pushing against the mighty river proved exhausting to Skein. He had to surface once more. As he did so, he struck an object. It was the shuffler he'd dove in to save! Stitcher grabbed her about the waist and swam upward. He surfaced again, pulling the unresponsive woman with him. He breathed in deeply and looked to the shore. He turned to see the steamer coming right at him. Stitcher swam toward the riverbank. The riverboat slowed and turned. It narrowly missed Stitcher in the water. Mr. Ague fired ineffectually as Stitcher reached the shore and set the shuffler on the ground.

"Get him!" Ague shouted to the shuffler. "You must obey my orders!"

The shuffler turned toward Skein. With her eyes pooled with vapidity and arm extended, she moved slowly toward him.

Stitcher backed away from the woman. She tilted her head to the side; her face affected a strangely alluring expression while her eyes remained empty. Driven forward by purely mechanical motion, she met Stitcher with an embrace.

Stitcher did not resist as she draped her creamy arms around his neck. His awareness of the unnaturalness of the attraction did not stop him from leaning in to accept her proffered lips to his own. He managed to break the spell when her lips pressed into his mask. He grabbed her shoulders, gently yet firmly pushing her away.

Letting out a scream, the shuffler resisted Skein. Without relenting, he continued to move her back. He rushed away from her into the grove of trees. She pursued in a steady, lurching walk. He drew the Embalmizer gun and released the gas from its nozzle. She staggered and fell to the ground.

Ague watched as the pair disappeared. "After them!" he ordered. Obediently, the shufflers moved down the gangplank.

Skein grabbed the woman around her svelte waist, slinging her over his shoulder in the same motion. He rushed away through the grove. The sound of shufflers followed them. The creatures broke branches in their path and filled the air with woeful moans.

❧ ❧ ❧

"I said they'd move," Officer Harbow said as he drove along. "Cattle are the same way–you get a cow in the road, you just tap 'er lightly with the jalopy's bumper."

Tom rolled his eyes. "It's really not how we'd do it in Chicago. It sure worked, but if it hadn't, we'd've had a mess."

"Oh yeah?" Al replied. "This is Louisiana, not Illinois. We do things different down here, Yank."

"You can stop calling me a Yank, Harbow. I'm a Northerner, but Yankee's more for Coasters. We're not all alike up North."

Al shrugged. "Sure. We're not all alike down here, either."

Tom sighed. "Okay. Let's just truce it. Where're we headed?"

Al nodded through the Cyprus grove at the abandoned mansion. "That's the old Smelt Estate. It's been out of commission since the states war. Some Jayhawkers came through and ransacked the place while Mister Smelt was off fighting for the Confederacy."

"There's some smoke coming from it!" Tom replied.

"Damn! So there is!" Al squinted. "Looks like dust from here. Let's check it out."

Al steered the sedan down the vine-choked dirt road. Off to their left, they saw several people weaving through the trees. The shuffling group chased after Skein. The latter carried an unconscious woman slung over his shoulders. Al raised his hat to scratch his head. "What the heck is going on, Barrett?"

"Search me," Barrett replied. "Looks like Skein could use help. Let's go."

Al and Tom got out of the car to aid Skein. "Skein!" Barrett shouted, waving his hands in the air. "Skein! Over here!"

Skein turned his head toward the officers. He deftly rushed between a group four shufflers coming the other way.

"Why'd you come this way?" Officer Harbow asked. "We were going to help you fight them off."

Skein headed toward their car. "Take this woman to a hospital. Handcuff her. She is dangerous."

Officer Barrett rushed after him. "Wait a minute! I don't know what's going on, but we've gotta nip it in the bud!"

"You need to get her to the hospital NOW!" Skein turned to face the shufflers. "I'll take care of this."

Skein opened the back door to the sedan. The air from the swamp cooler washed over him as he laid the woman gently on the seat. As he did so, a shuffler opened the handle to the door to other side of the car. Stitcher pulled his gas gun and fired it.

The shuffler stumbled against the door frame in a coughing fit. Officer Harbow came around the front of the sedan and drew his revolver. He aimed his gun at the shuffler.

"Al, don't!" shouted Tom, coming around the back of the car. "Don't shoot!"

"Please," the shuffler coughed, "please don't shoot me!"

Al pointed his gun to the ground. "He's recovering from whatever's wrong with him!" He turned to Skein. "How did that happen?"

Skein looked into the police sedan. He pointed at the bullet-shaped swamp chiller. "How's that thing work?"

Harbow shrugged. "No idea. I put in gas. I start it up. We drive. It cools the inside of the car."

Skein looked the car at the coughing shuffler. "The chiller changes the chemicals in the gas. It loosens Ague's hold!" Skein rushed around the car. Pulling the chiller from its perch in the door, he shattered the glass.

"Hey!" Al protested.

Skein looked at the officer. "Take the woman to the hospital. From the sound of her breathing, she is no longer enthralled."

He turned to meet the shufflers crawling from the drainage ditch. He shoved the nozzle of the gas gun into the swamp chiller as some fifty shufflers approached. They staggered and stumbled. They roared throaty moans.

The car started. "Are you going to be okay?" Officer Barrett shouted out the window. "You can ask if you need help."

"Good idea," Skein shouted. He pulled the cord the air conditioner. It thrummed to life.

The high-pitched squeal of the machine sent the creatures into a frenzy. Rushing at Skein, they howled with an unholy intensity. Pointing the air conditioner at the shufflers, Skein released a short whiff of gas into it.

The gas rushed out at high velocity and fanned out. Six of the shufflers fell coughing to the road. More came behind them. Skein fired the Embalmizer into the port of the air conditioner. It distributed a wide swath of the gas through the shufflers. He reloaded a cartridge as a new mob of shufflers headed toward him, but they moved too quickly.

Skein moved with the smooth motions of a leopard. His feet and fists struck out in symphonic harmony. The powerhouse of a man waded through rows of the shufflers, carpeting the ground with their writhing forms as they attempted to regain their footing. Despite the admirable effort, Stitcher succumbed to the brute force of numbers and fell beneath the combined weight of some thirty shufflers. He ceased struggling, yet his muscles remained tensed, steel cords.

The shufflers climbed off him, parting in lines to the side. Three burly shufflers held tight to his arms and pulled him to his feet. Another shuffler carried the bullet-shaped chiller away.

In the center of the parted lines strode the figure of Ague. "Ah, it is 'Skein', is it not? The moniker challenges me to avoid laughter! I am so glad to find you in this manner!"

Stitcher gritted his teeth. Hate seethed from his eyes. "Enjoy it. You won't find me like this again. If I find you like this, I won't spend time playing 'ring around the rosie'."

Ague mockingly clapped his hands together. "Oh, isn't that quaint? You presume you will ever be free again! Perhaps it is time we see under the mask."

Skein turned his head away, struggling against his bonds. Instead of approaching, Ague began to pull at his own nose. "No, you ridiculous man. I know who you are. I wish to show you who I am, before you die."

Stitcher gasped and let out a moan as the makeup peeled away. The face of Lucille rested beneath the mask. Stitcher fell limp in the arms of the shufflers. "Lucille! NO! Why?"

"Because," her luscious lips said, "you have power to speak with the dead. That power is power that I want."

"You know," Stitcher snarled, "that my girl has my heart, and can have anything that is in my power to give her." His muscles tensed and pulled the shufflers forward and over his head. The largest headed right for Lucille. "You can't fool me, damn you!"

Lucille's image faded as the shuffler went through it. Skein fought like a madman. His rage pressed him through the shufflers as he retrieved the Embalmizer. "I'm coming for you, Ague!"

He quickly reloaded the Embalmizer. He used it in short bursts to stave off approaching shufflers as he headed for the river. More shufflers came from upstream.

"Where do you think those came from?" a voice said.

Stitcher shrugged. "Don't know," he replied. "Who are you?"

"Does it really matter?"

Stitcher sighed between hard breaths. "Oh. It's you, Plume. Go to hell. Let me do what I need to do."

"Maybe I've been there, Gleaves. Maybe I haven't."

Stitcher rushed between trees to see the riverboat moored to the shore.

"You're a weasel, a liar, and a traitor Plume. I was going to take you in. I shot you with my gasgun right before that mustard-gas attack hit. Got out of there when the artillery hit. Never recovered a body, but didn't much care. Just another unknown in the mud. More'n you deserved."

"Wow-you really hate me, doncha Stitcher? Maybe I was gonna help you out? Maybe I won't now."

"Knock it off, Plume. You wouldn't be talkin' if you didn't have something to say. Don't know what rules you have to play by on that side, but you wouldn't do me any favors. Cough it up."

A heavy sigh dusted Stitcher's ears. "That's rude to say. You know how I died."

"I wasn't all that sorry for a guy taking money from a Kraut spy on troop positions. So, you got caught in what they bought. A lot of my friends died in that attack." Skein ran toward the riverboat's gangplank. "You weren't one of them."

"Alright Stitcher. You got me. I've got to tell you."

"Tell me in a minute." Skein rushed at the two burly shufflers guarding the end of the gangplank. With a swift kick to the nearest, he sent it staggering into the second.

Skein observed the shuffler guards still trying to regain their footing as he rushed up the gangplank. He pulled his revolver and fired it into the mooring rope tied to a tree. The gangplank landed with a splash against the water.

Skein turned to the boat and shouted, "Ague! I know you're here, you bastard! Last four seconds of the fourth quarter, fourth down, and you got the pigskin! Let's get this damn game of yours over with!" Only the sounds of the river responded. "You have my dad and my girl, and I'll have your life if you don't give them back!"

"Fine, Mister Gleaves." Skein looked to the second deck of the riverboat. Ague stood there, with his arms around blank-eyed Lucille and his blank-eyed father, Joseph Gleaves. "Here they are, Skein. You can have them, if you insist. Come and get them."

Ague's face twisted in a wicked, broad smile. "All you have to do is get past my blockers to tackle me." Lucille and Joe stepped in front of Ague. He placed a mechanical device around Lucille's neck, the placed an identical one around the neck of Joe Gleaves. "These are bombs," Ague said. "If you touch the device itself, it will be the end of you, of your future, of your past. Or, Skein, you can give me what I want."

"What do you want?"

"I want," Ague paused dramatically before continuing. "I want the secret to speaking with the dead."

Stitcher stood up. "You want that? I'd give it to you if I could. It's a goddamn curse!"

"Give it to me, Jacob."

"I told you, I can't!"

Mister Ague chortled. "Since you discover it impossible to fulfill a simple request, you win. Come and get your prizes." The strange figure turned to leave, walking by a pair of large alligators, eying the figures of Joe Gleaves and Lucille.

"No!" Skein ascended the staircases three at a time until he reached the second deck. Pulling his revolver he rushed after the first gator. He fired into its head. Turning on him, the eyes of the reptile glowed with unnatural knowing and malevolence.

Skein stood his ground. The gator leapt at him. He kicked the gator in the side as it flew by, knocking it over the edge of the boat. He heard a splash in the churning river below as he turned to deal with the other gator. He saw it leap toward, and bite deeply into, the midsection of his beloved Lucille. "NO!"

🐛 🐛 🐛

Driving toward town, Al turned down the street. It being late afternoon, people walked around town. "Do they seem a bit listless to you, Tom?"

Officer Barrett nodded in reply. "Just like those folks in the country. It must be connected, Al."

Officer Harbow scratched his head. "Without Skein's gas we oughta avoid a crowd scene. It's time we figured out how they get this way."

Tom looked at the woman sleeping in the back of the car. "We need to get to the nearest hospital."

Al scratched his head. "There's a small asylum just down the road, not far from the old Smelt Plantation. We can try there but it's for whites."

"If we can try there," Officer Barrett replied, "They'll take care of her, or I'll take care of them."

Harbow turned the sedan at the crossroad, driving toward the mansion that appeared in the distance.

As they pulled into the courtyard, they saw it filled with people dressed in nightclothes who wandering about in a daze. Harbow slowed the sedan and drove forward cautiously. "Are they shufflers?"

Barrett shrugged. "This is an asylum, so they could be patients. They aren't making moves to attack us."

"The shufflers don't seem to attack unless provoked."

"Or ordered."

Harbow nodded. He pulled the sedan up to the mansion's granite steps. People wandered aimlessly around the porch.

Barrett turned the door handle. Harbow grabbed his partner's arm. "Wait a sec, Tom. We need to have our guns ready. We might just set off a hornet's nest."

Nodding, Barrett pulled his gun. "What if some of these people are shufflers and some are not?"

"We don't want to shoot anyone, shuffler or not. We've still got to be ready for anything. Try not to set 'em off. Let's go." Harbow opened his door cautiously. After retrieving the woman from the backseat and slinging her over his shoulder, Barrett pulled his gun as well.

People wandered by them as if they were not there. Moving past the wanderers, Barrett followed Harbow into the mansion.

"This is creepy," Barrett said. "Can't tell if they're shufflers, or if they just have something wrong with them."

Harbow cleared his throat as they reached the door. "Yeah. An asylum's a perfect place to work with zombies. Shufflers look just like patients."

The entryway to the asylum contained fewer wanderers. Officer Harbow walked to the reception desk. "I'm a police officer. This woman is injured and needs a doctor."

The trim woman in a nurse uniform looked at Harbow over her glasses and pursed her lips. "We are not a hospital."

Barrett came forward and kicked the desk. The nurse moved away as he used an arm to sweep away the stack of papers on the desk. He laid the woman on the desk. "The heck you're not! If you don't find a doctor, I'll look for one!"

The nurse stood up. "What are the stakes, Officer? I am the head nurse. We do not treat people who walk in demanding help!"

"Calm down Barrett!" Harbow said. He turned back to the nurse. "I'm sorry, ma'am. This woman needs treatment, or she could die. He's from Chi Town. He doesn't know how we work here."

"I know how people should work everywhere," Barrett mumbled.

The nurse smiled darkly. "Oh? She needs treatment." She reached in her pocket and pulled out a scalpel. "Why didn't you say so?" She plunged the scalpel toward the woman.

"NO!" Harbow's gun flashed and banged, the bullet plunging into the nurse's arm. The nurse seemed affected only by the physical force of the bullet as it forced her against the wall. The nurse smiled. She came at Harbow with the scalpel, plunging it into his chest. He fell to the floor in shock as blood streamed from the wound.

"Oh God!" Barrett said, his eyes widened. "You're insane!" The nurse turned to rush at him. He fired at her. She jolted under the impact of the bullets as she continued forward to knock him to the ground. Blood dripped from her bullet wounds as she straddled his chest. She smiled. "Call it what you will, darling." Barrett could not move. Leaning forward, she gave him a passionate kiss on the lips. She smiled as she moved away. "Now we can be together forever." Barrett's eyes stared blankly into the distance.

Seeing Lucille torn in two by the jaws of the gator, Skein fell to his knees.

"You FOOL!" Skein looked up to see Lucille standing there as the illusions of his father and the gator faded away. "Now you know that you cannot protect what you love from me?"

Stitcher stood to attention. "You will see that I will resist you to my last breath. I swear to kill you, Devil!"

Lucille laughed. Her laugh was vicious and cruel. "It is too easy, is it not, to think I am the Devil? To think I am not your precious Lucille?" Lucille held her arm out. "Come, then. Touch my skin. Judge my flesh to see if I am illusion or reality."

Removing the glove from his right hand, Skein moved forward slowly. His fingers quavered as he touched Lucille's warm, naked, living, warm, soft arm. Unsure, he brought his fingers to her cheek. He ran his thumb over her moist, ruby lips.

"NO!" He backed away from her.

She nodded. "Yes. You know, now, that it is true."

"How? Ague?"

Lucille smiled. "You still do not realize, do you? 'Mister Ague', Prêtre Ague, the owner of the Plantation abandoned in the Civil War, and I. We are all the same person."

"How?"

"How, you ask? I have come back. I incarnate in many forms, with one purpose; to resist Heaven. Lucille is my latest form."

*She came at Harbow with the scalpel...*

Stitcher let his arms fall to his side and his glove to the deck. "I do not understand."

"Of course you do not," Lucille's lips dripped the venomous words. "Humans do not wish to believe in the Devil, because that would mean there is a God. They don't want to believe there is a God because he will not show them miracles." Lucille waved her beautiful arms about to indicate the beauty of the bayou. "Is not this a collection of untold miracles?" "They believe in me because I show them lies and trickery to amuse them. I show them this because it amuses me. They ask why their god kills, maims, destroys. God has the sense to not give the accusations the dignity of a reply. I give people faith in hatred, illusion, pain, in darkness. All the tangibles of this existence. He gives nothing."

"No," Stitcher replied, "he gives them love. There is nothing else to give. Why do you hate him so much?"

"That is the irony, I love him, yet he will not give himself to me alone. That is why I hate him."

"Seem to hold a high opinion for yourself. If he'd love only you," Skein replied, "it would not be love. He could not be God."

Lucille turned with a sneer. "He could be my God! Mine alone!" Lucille hissed. "Is that not enough? Am I not enough?"

Stitcher removed his mask and gloves to grasp her arms in a powerful grip. "You are enough for me Lucille. I don't see evil in you. By some demon or spirit you're possessed. I love you, Lucille, beyond the lie possessing you."

Lucille's eyes blinked rapidly. Her eyes stopped blinking and looked at Skein. "Stitcher? I love you."

A voice came to Stitcher's ear. "She's lying to you."

Stitcher shook his head. "She's not. I know her eyes. You are the liar."

The ghost sighed. "She's still possessed."

"Possessed by whom?"

"By Plume."

"What?"

"Your mistake, Gleaves, was in assuming your foe was a living man. That's why we came to help you."

Skein replaced his mask. "I will kill him."

"He's a ghost. He cannot be killed."

"I don't believe that."

"Believe what you will. I'll tell you one more thing," the ghastly voice whispered. "He wants you out of his way. He doesn't need this boat. He has others he'll use. A time-bomb is planted on this boat. It will go off in less than a minute. You have no time to escape."

Skein let go of Lucille's hand. "We'll see." Grasping the railing with both hands, he swung backwards over it, letting his momentum carry him in an arc. Letting go, he swung through the air. Momentum and gravity carried him to the bottom deck. Landing on his feet, he rushed to his motorcycle. He disentangled it from the railing with a yank. He leapt on the bike and struck the pedal with his foot. The motor thrummed to life. With uncanny skill and speed, he rode the motorcycle up the luggage ramp.

On the second deck, he drove the bike hard to a stop at Lucille's side, swinging her onto the back of the bike. She wrapped her arms around Skein's waist as he gunned the engine and rode it up the ramp to the roof.

Seeing shore, Skein quickly gauged the distance and pushed the cycle to its limits. Pieces of the tar roof flew into the air as the back wheel spun violently against it. The bike built up speed, heading for the end of the steamboat.

The motorcycle flew off the edge of the roof as an explosion rocked the boat, pushing the bike forward with violence. Stitcher fought the handlebars as the motorcycle glided toward shore.

The bike struck the silted beach, sending a spray of soft mud into the air. The momentum threw Stitcher and Lucille forward to sink in a mass of soft muck.

Stitcher stood in the green slime, wiping it off the ports of his gasmask. His vision clear, he saw his revolver pointed at his face.

"So, you didn't believe me before?" Lucille smiled wickedly. "Perhaps I might convince you yet."

Skein stared from behind his mask. He walked forward as he watched Lucille's finger drag the trigger back slowly. The gun clicked as he took it from her hand. "If the bullet had gone off," Stitcher said, shaking mud out of the barrel, "you would have blown your hand to pieces."

Lucille rushed at him, her fingernails slashing at his mask.

Stitcher grasped her wrists. She spat and kicked at him. "Stop this! Throwing a tantrum won't get you anywhere! I'm starting to think you are possessed by the Devil." He sighed. "I've got to get to the asylum. I'll have to restrain you."

Lucille calmed down. She looked at Skein's mask. Tears formed in her eyes. "Use your gasgun on me," she said. "You can't take me with you. I'm not myself." She put her arms around his neck. "I'm scared Stitch!"

Stitcher nodded. Backing away from Lucille's embrace, he pulled his gasgun and switched out the cartridge. He lifted his gasmask to gently kiss Lucille's mud-covered lips. "I don't understand what's happening to you Lucille. You're not like the shufflers, as far as I can tell." When the kiss was over, he placed his gasmask on and backed away. "I know I love you, Lucille. I'll get you help when this is over."

Lucille closed her eyes. "I love you too."

The green smoke from the gasgun enveloped Lucille. Stitcher grabbed her as she fell toward the ground. He gently laid her down to lean against a cypress tree. "If that's you in there, Plume; I'm going to kill you for what you've done to her."

Walking to the motorcycle to extricate it from the wet mud and pulled it onto the sandy shore. He went into the river and took a clothed bath. Once clean, he pulled the machine into the river to wash away the mud.

"It's not going to run," a voice whispered. "The engine's been in the water."

Stitcher pulled the bike out again. "I had to run it through worse in the Great War. I installed special seals so water wouldn't leave me stranded in the middle of a battlefied." Stitcher pushed to motorcycle over to Lucille's unconscious body. He rested the motorcycle against the tree. He gently lifted her as he mounted the motorcycle, grasping the handle bars under her cradled form.

"Are you going to ride like that?" the voice asked. "Why don't you get her later?"

"The swamp is home to gators, snakes, and predators. I'm done talking to you now."

"Plume knows you're coming."

He sat on the motorcycle and kicked the pedals. The bike roared to life. "I won't disappoint him." Skein rode through the swamp toward the asylum.

Carefully following trails through the swamp and testing the capacity of rotting bridges and planks over streams, swamps and ponds both wet and dry, Skein made good time. Soon, the three stories of the asylum's white-washed outer walls and pillars rose as beacons against the oncoming twilight. He stopped to rest Lucille against a tree. "I know it's not the best place to leave you. I can't take you with me." He looked at the asylum's porch, barely visible through the dense foliage.

The modified Excelsior motorcycle hummed quietly as it moved toward the sanitarium. In the fading light, Skein stopped the motorcycle to watch the proceedings in the asylum's courtyard. The people inside shuffled aimlessly and listlessly to and fro. All moved in silence, neither speaking to one another nor yet to themselves. The residents of the complex congregated about the porch. The setting sun offered eerie reflections from their eyes.

Their necks snapped suddenly to stare piercingly and directly at Skein in his obscured place between the flora's dense thickets. The sky darkened slightly to coincide with the sudden movement.

Skein continued watching the figures on the porch. Not a one of them moved an inch as their eyes continued staring. He tilted his body and the motorcycle to his left as an experiment. All of the people tilted their heads in unison. He returned his motorcycle to its upright position. All the eyes followed him with precision.

Removing his gasgun from its holster with his left hand, he opened the snap covering the revolver's hammer with his right.

"Still not using your revolver?" Skein turned to see Lucille standing behind him. She held her hands coyly behind her back. The sundress tickled her thighs in the slight, warm swamp breeze. She displayed her teeth in a broad alligator smile. Her eyes glowed with a reddish hue, duplicating the shufflers stare. "Some of them are dead, you know."

Her tone was so matter-of-fact, it gave Skein pause. "Is my father…"

Lucille laughed in a hollow, wicked tone. "Is your father dead? Possibly. Is he over there? He stands on the lawn. Look!"

Skein didn't take his eyes off of Lucille. "He is there. I saw him with the others. You said some are dead?"

Lucille shrugged her shoulders. "Some are. They don't live forever, you know. They starve to death unless forced to eat. When they die, that's when they realize they're hungry."

Skein tensed. "Who are you?"

"Perhaps you must be shown."

Skein looked at the asylum. "I'll find the truth in there."

"You will know Hell, Stitcher Gleaves!"

"If that's what it takes." Skein didn't turn. He pointed the gun and released a stream of gas from its nozzle. He heard her fall softly to the loamy earth. "We'll work this out when I get back from the sanitarium." He rolled his shoulders in a stretch. He put the motorcycle in gear, riding it slowly toward the mental hospital.

The shufflers snapped their necks at each slight change in the motorcycle's movements, never taking their eyes off of him. The stuttered motions they made created the appearance of a film.

"It's enough to give a cemetery night watchman the jitters."

"Getting unnerved?" a voice asked over his shoulder.

"Not at all," Skein replied. "After the dead and maimed bodies I saw in the war and in the motordromes, I don't get nerves. Nothing shocks me anymore."

The voice laughed. "Might be an eye-opener; even for Skein."

"Is that so? Eyes're gonna be saucer-sized when I'm done."

"These shufflers won't pull any punches with you, Stitcher."

"Ten-to-one's just fine betting odds. If they go all-out, it'll make an even playing field."

Skein rode the roaring motorcycle forward, increasing speed as he approached the closed gates. He lifted the front tire slightly off the ground and braced for impact.

The wheel slammed into the iron gates, pushing them apart with extreme violence. The gates slammed hard against the fence. Skein rode the cycle toward the gathering of shufflers. The latter continued to watch his progress with staccato-like, neck jerk movements. He rode through the crowd of shufflers at breakneck speed, kicking aside those who got in his way.

Reacting to his attacks, the shufflers rushed toward him. He narrowly slipped between the barriers of human bodies. He side-swiped one of the muscled male shufflers. The blow knocked the shuffler violently to the ground. Rapidly climbing the steps, the motorcycle crashed through the doors.

The Skein stopped the motorcycle just inside the lobby. Turning the machine off, a tranquil scene greeted the hero's vision. The shufflers stood behind him, but would not enter.

Sitting at the desk, an attractive, blonde nurse pushed up her glasses as she to look at Skein. "May I help you?" she asked.

The Skein stepped off the bike. "You may," he replied. "I'm not sure you're gonna."

The woman stood. Blood coated the hem of her nurse's skirt. "Until I know what you want, I can't help you."

The Skein pulled his pistol. "I think you know why I'm here. Maybe even better than I do."

"Sir!" The nurse rushed to attack him.

The Skein pulled the trigger on his gasgun as a stream of green gas corrupted the air.

The woman rushed forward, her mouth filling with the cloud of gas. He struck the woman on the temple with the butt of the gasgun. The woman took no notice of the bleeding wound it made. Her mouth remained open wide. No sound came from her lips. Green vapors trailed from her open maw. She lashed at The Skein with her manicured nails, scraping over his gasmask. She gripped the mask in her fingers, pulling at its base. The Skein pushed at her violently. She fell backwards, pulling the mask off The Skein's head. The noxious fumes of his own creation filled his lungs. He stumbled. He pursued after his attacker, still carrying the mask. He fell unconscious to the ground.

A curious sound rang in his ears. Two hands rhythmically beat against each other. Mr. Ague came into his view. Laughing, the man or monster applauded Skein's defeat. Stitcher couldn't move or respond.

When The Skein once more opened his eyes, ropes stretched his arms and legs wide between two pillars high above the porch of the Smelt Mansion. The Skein's body formed an 'x'. Below him, Mr. Rotten laughed as flames crawled voraciously up the pillars. "The great Skein is unraveled! There is no way out for you. I want to direct your attention to the line of zombies in the distance."

Stitcher looked up to see a long train of zombies walking single-file through the swamp. Mister Ague laughed again. "I have ordered them to walk into the river. As an honorific to your family, the one leading the conga line is your own father." Mr. Ague looked up and smiled broadly. "He helped put you where you are today. He did so at my insistence, of course."

Clenching his teeth, Stitcher watched the long shadows of the zombies. "If they die," he vowed, "you will die as well!"

"Come along now," Mr. Ague returned. "You still do not know me?"

Stitcher nodded. "I know who you claim to be. You claim to be, or think you are, the father of lies." Stitcher laughed out loud. "If you truly are, you missed your biggest lie! It doesn't take long for a liar to start believing them. Why should I take your word on anything? Whoever you are, and I know who you are, Plume, what a joke you are!"

Mister Ague sighed. "Perhaps. Still, you're up there. Powerless is what you are, and who you are."

"Just another lie!" Stitcher looked toward the sky. "I have access to power you can't imagine." He closed his eyes. After a moment, he opened them again. His muscles tensed under his uniform. His neck muscles strained with violence. The ropes dug into Stitcher's gloves as he pulled against them.

Mr. Ague laughed. "Do you really think you can escape? A regular

Sampson, I suppose?"

"Yeah, Stitcher," a voice came from behind him. "You're stuck! You can't think you're gonna break those ropes!"

The Skein's voice came as a lion's roar. "I don't think a damned thing! I know!"

Skein kept up the pressure on his muscles. Slowly, tiny threads began to snap in succession.

Mr. Ague looked up at the popping sounds. "What the hell?"

Blood appeared on Skein's face, dripping down with his profuse sweat. Strands of rope came undone with snapping sounds.

"Stop it!"

The flames reached the soles of his boots, helping to weaken the ropes around his legs while threatening to injure him. The rope around his right leg snapped first. "I'm gonna make a liar out of both of you!" he shouted.

Mr. Ague put his hand to his mouth.

The Skein swung to his body toward his left, adding strain to the rope around his right arm as the flames licked at it. "Just hope those ropes or your lies protect you, Ague!"

The rope around his right hand snapped. The Skein swung violently against the pillar on his left side. He brought his right hand to the utility belt he wore. Though gloved, his fingers effortlessly retrieved a knife from one of the satchels.

Below, Mr. Ague produced a small sphere and tossed it. It struck Stitcher as he sawed at the rope around his leg. The pellet bounced off and fell into the flaming inferno below.

His leg free, The Skein turned his attention and his knife to the rope around his left arm. He looked below him, the porch intensely aflame. Black smoke escaped the conflagration. The rope gave away. He plunged straight toward the blaze below. A puff of sparks and flame shot upward, garnering an uncontrolled glee from Mr. Ague. "The death of Skein!" Ague laughed.

Mr. Ague watched as the flames parted away. He stared as Skein strode through the engulfing fire, wearing his gasmask. The remnant of the ropes around his gloved wrists disintegrated in the fervent heat.

"NO!" Ague shouted. "NO! IT CAN'T BE!"

The Skein laughed harshly. "You lied to yourself, Ague!" He rushed forward, grasping the fiend's neck with his right hand. The Skein forced Ague to the ground with the latter clutching at the throttling hand. "You lied to yourself when you said to yourself you couldn't be defeated! I've put you in the dirt, where vermin belongs. Call the shufflers back, or I'll plow you under it."

"I am not defeated!" Ague gasped.

"Are you going to keep lying to yourself until it kills you? If you don't call them back, it will kill you. I will kill you!"

Ague's body thinned and elongated, turning a sickly green color. His mouth widened and gaped to reveal slathering fangs. His eyeteeth jutted and narrowed, as did his eyes. Ague transformed himself into a large, hissing, poisonous viper.

Momentarily surprised, The Skein stepped back, yet maintained his grip. "You're an accomplished mesmerist, Plume. I'll grant you that. If you were really a snake, you'd have bitten me already. I'm losing my patience. Call back the swamp shufflers. I know I can kill you now. Do you really think I won't? I know that, whether you're the devil or a man, your body is a man's. Are you sure you're immortal? I'm willing to let my money ride on the number I've picked. How 'bout you?"

The snake twisted in the air, failing in its attempt to loosen Skein's hold. "Damn you, Stitcher Gleaves! Damn you!"

"Yes," Skein laughed. "Damn me, but save yourself!" With his free hand, the Skein pulled the snake up until they were at eye level. "I came ready to die. I came ready to fail. Did you? You can bite me right now. Do it. Fourth down, snake. Are you gonna throw the ball or punt? Call the swamp shufflers back, Plume!"

The snake's smile broadened. "I already did."

The Skein watched as swamp shufflers came out of the trees and waded through the muck and swamp. More than he'd seen until now. Perhaps thousands. They came, their pale skin scratched and bleeding. Their eyes glowered with hatred. They rushed The Skein as the mansion burned behind him.

Skein strangled the snake. As the illusion of the shufflers faded Ague again donned human appearance, his eyes wide from lack of oxygen. He tried to cough, but could not. "Still punting, Plume?"

Ague held his hands up in surrender. The Skein released the pressure on his adversary's neck. "Talk."

"I can't call them back when they are out of my range. If I had your ability to speak with the dead, I could. I have a radio device in my pocket for longer distances. Can I get it?"

The Skein lifted Ague into the air. He shuffled through the jacket pockets until he found a five-inch-cube of a wooden box. Painted black, the box had an unmarked knob on it. He examined it before turning the knob. The box made a continuous droning sound. The Skein stared toward the swamp where the shufflers disappeared earlier. "They'll come back?"

Ague nodded. "They will return."

Skein turned to the swamp. Shufflers arrived from the thick trees, bedraggled and bewildered.

The Skein turned back to Ague, tightening his grip. "You got any more tricks, rat?"

"Just one, for now." The Skein turned around to see that he held his Lucille in an iron grip. He let go of her quickly and dropped to his knees to hold her. He pulled off his mask. "What did you make me do, Plume?"

"I merely tested your mettle," Ague said, as he appeared ten yards away. "I wished to see if you could kill me." The villain laughed. "You could not. And you thought I was the dead one! Lucille will be fine."

Stitcher stood and walked toward Ague. "Be assured Plume; I've it in me to kill you. You can bet on it." He clenched his fists. "In fact..."

A hand fell on his shoulder, staying him. Stitcher turned to see his father. "Leave it be, son." Joe Gleaves glared at Ague. "He's infectious." The shufflers moved toward Mr. Ague.

"NO!" Ague shouted, retreating toward the burning mansion. "Get back! Stay away!" His face melted like wax, revealing the pale, pasty and burned features of Plume.

"Shufflers have no mind of their own." Stitcher's father reminded. "Your illusions will not affect them, Plume. You've got nothin' left but your rotten lies." Joe shook his head. "You're defenseless without them. You can't hurt us anymore."

Mr. Ague rushed through the burning doorway, pursued by the shufflers. Slowly, Joseph Gleaves followed after them.

"Don't go in there, Pops!" Stitcher said. "Get those people to safety! It's on fire! You'll all be killed!"

Joseph Gleaves turned to his son. "Not to be morbid, son, but none of us can die again. We starved to death days ago. Shuffling can drain a person in a few hours. Ague only fed those he thought were important." He turned to the flames. The reflections danced over his face. "We're here for retribution. Mister Ague, or Plume as you knew him, is gonna die tonight. Those you shot with the chiller were infectious, and freed the others like wildfire. The man you saved at the police car told us all about it." He walked slowly to the entrance. "Know that I love you, Stitcher. Take care of Lucille. She'll make you a fine wife. Make her a better husband." With that, Joseph Gleaves turned to the flames, his shadow stretching in the firelight, and followed Ague into the blaze.

Lucille moaned, returning Stitcher's attention. He rushed to her side.

He knelt beside her, cradling her head in his arms. "Are you okay, Lucille?"

Lucille coughed. She nodded. "I'm alright, Stitcher. Just take me home."

Stitcher picked her up and carried her. As he walked away, the mansion fell. It spewed forth unholy sounds, sparks and smoke. The deafening roar of the immolation cut the night air.

Two shufflers, still wandering in a daze approached Skein. "Officers Harbow and Barrett!" he said. "How are you two?"

Barrett shook his head. "Don't know about Harbow, but I'm ready to go back North. And, I'm hungry. Gangsters are the scariest thing there. Glad to not be in a daze."

"And taxes," Harbow put in. The officer looked at the wandering shufflers and the burning mansion. "We'll get this under wraps, Skein. You go home."

Skein nodded. "Thanks fellas." He put his arm around Lucille. "Come on honey. It's over now. Let's go home."

Stitcher barely heard the ghostly voice. "It's over for now, Jacob Moses Gleaves. Stitcher. You can rest for now, but you cannot rest for long. The Skein is not yet complete."

Stitcher nodded as he walked Lucille to his motorcycle.

# THE END

# BIRTH OF THE SKEIN

Having seen the film, The Emperor Jones, I became fascinated with the African American singer (for whom the song Old Man River was written), actor, peace and civil rights activist, college football hero etc., Paul Robeson. I thought Paul seemed very much a hero to me. Strangely, Paul Robeson was mentioned in the biography of the British writer, Olaf Stapledon. When two heroes of mine cross paths in unexpected ways, I find it difficult to ignore. When addressing the life of Jacob Moses "Stitcher" Gleaves, it became a matter of wonder at how closely the lives of these two figures paralleled each other and yet their stories grew so divergent. This story, however, deals with the singular figure of Mr. Gleaves, whose history is not so well known as the illustrious Mr. Robeson's, so I will let those interested learn more about Robeson for themselves. He is just an one example of the many people of African descent I admire greatly.

Growing up poor and a bit out-of-place in a struggling mining town in Montana, I learned a bit about struggle and prejudice. My first television memory was seeing David Carradine appear as he walked over a sand dune. I wasn't old enough to know who he was or what Kung Fu meant, but I liked the fact that the hero came from a mysterious place far away. This type of hero stayed with me throughout my life, and set me on appreciating heroes different from me in color. Certainly, I still thought Bionic Man was cool, but even Lee Majors' character was a bit of an outcast and overcame much. I recall reading Black Lightning and Ragman, who were again limited by their social standing. This and television movies, *Roots,* replays of *Defiant Ones* and recorded speeches of Martin Luther King informed me a little about what the experience of being African American meant. I couldn't suggest I fully understand, but I can say I want to understand and be supportive of the rights of all mankind.

When I realized there were no African American pulp heroes, (a fact now rectified by the awesome writings of Charles Saunders (*Damballa*) and Derrick Ferguson's very cool Mongrel (included in this volume), I wanted to pay tribute to and explore the experience that had so inspired my own. I think it's difficult to avoid mentioning in pulp history THE SHADOW's agent, JERICHO JONES, and the interesting stories, part true, part legend, DEADWOOD DICK from the days of the Old West.

Jacob 'Moses' Gleaves is informed by the rich history of New Orleans and Louisiana. The contribution of American musical genius from the area cannot be denied. Jelly Roll Morton played on the stereo while I wrote. In telling The Skein's story, I relied on many friends. I'd like to thank Mike Indest for informing me about the history of New Orleans and the area, Gabriel Offutt for our discussions on Catholicism, and Bob Calkins for proof-reading the finished story and offering great suggestions and impressions.

I know I have not spoken at length about Jacob Moses "Stitcher" Gleaves, or The Skein himself, yet I hope his life unfolds satisfactorily throughout the story and will continue to do so in the future volumes. For me, I have to admit he is a man that I cannot pretend to fully understand, and may never be able to do so. He certainly fascinates and inspires me. I hope he does the same for you.


KEVIN NOEL OLSON - lives in Butte, Montana, where once lived the writer and erstwhile Pinkerton agent, Dashiell Hammett. To date, Mister Olson has written nine books, including the middle-grade Tocsin Codex Trilogy about a young girl named Eerey Tocsin and her strange adventures with her unusual family and friends. He has also appeared in several anthologies as well as having poetry published in The Masonic Society journal and sundry articles. His greatest and most fulfilling accomplishment was marrying up, as it were, and managing to maintain a great, loving relationship with his wife, Amelinda.

# THE BROWN RECLUSE

## "Web of the Brown Recluse"
### By Greg Gick

*February, 1935*

"**D**octor DuBois..."

The voice, silver and serpentine, seemed to be coming from very far away.

"*Doctor Emmanuel DuBois....*"

Even in his grogginess, it seemed to the thin, scholarly-looking man that he had heard that voice before. Somewhere. But he couldn't place it. His head was swimming too much for that.

"Doctor! Get up!"

After what seemed an eternity, Dr. Emmanuel DuBois managed to squint open his eyes and start to make sense of his surroundings. He seemed to be lying with his cheek against a cold, featureless metal floor. How did he get here? What did he remember? He had been coming out of the restaurant when the two burly men half in shadow had accosted him. Terrified he was being robbed, he had started to run away. But one of the men had reached out, holding something he couldn't see, and then it was as if a sudden electrical shock had jolted through his entire body. He had remembered no more.

The voice spoke again, this time with a weary sigh. "Pick him up." DuBois felt two heavy arms grasp his and haul him roughly to his feet. Everything swirled before his eyes. But through the kaleidoscope of waving color, he seemed to think he saw a number of white creampuffs he instantly identified as clouds. Clouds, in an azure sky that seemed to go on forever.

"Welcome to *The Spider's Eye*, Dr. DuBois," came the sibilant voice from behind him. "Please forgive the headache you undoubtedly must have. I was afraid my servants were forced to be rough."

As his senses slowly steadied, it came to DuBois that he was not lying somewhere on a Manhattan sidewalk as he should be. He was—he was on a ship of some kind. Somehow he knew he was moving, even though his body was standing still. And now he began to discern the low purring of engines. Was he on a boat? No....no. Not a boat. There was a ceiling over his head, made of the same gun-metal gray metal as the floor. And now he could see that the clouds were floating beyond a long, high pane of some sort of glass window, with no horizon in sight. He was in the *sky*. A plane, then? Still, no—they were moving much too slowly. A dirigible. That must be the answer. But how on earth did he get aboard a dirigible?

"Turn around, Doctor," the voice told him, as if reading his mind, "And all your questions will be answered."

DuBois saw that his arms were pinned by two of the largest, most thuggish men he had ever seen, doubtless the same two whom he had encountered….was it the night before? It was daylight now. Who were they? DuBois looked up at their faces…and immediately wished he hadn't.

They were the faces of the living dead.

The visages of his holders were the blankest, most totally non-emotional countenances a being could have and still be called human. They were utterly empty. No smiles, no frowns, barely a hint of life in them. Their eyes were dull and glazed, staring ahead of them in a ramrod straight line. It was if they weren't even noticing the man they clutched so tightly in their arms.

Curiously, the top of both men's head were covered completely with what seemed to be metallic skullcaps. DuBois had never seen the like.

The voice again: "Wondering about your captors, Doctor? I call them my Maton-Men. From 'automaton.' You see, that cap they're wearing completely controls their mind. A little invention I created. They no longer have any thoughts of their own; just what I tell them. Observe. Slaves, turn the captive to face me."

Upon the command, the two blank-faced men slowly but instantly began rotating DuBois around. The positive of his new position was now he could get a better view of where he was.

He *was* aboard a dirigible; on its very bridge, in fact. There could be no doubt. The room was shaped in a great circle, with the half behind him showcasing the great window that provided the view. The second half, however—that took DuBois' breath away.

For every square inch of the walls on the aft end of the bridge was made up of row upon row, bank upon bank, of the most advanced instrumentation DuBois had ever seen. Equipment so technical, so expensive, that even most government labs could not afford them. Yet here they were, and done up in such a compact, efficient method they could have fit in a college classroom.

Attending each machine were men with white coats and clipboards, each silently overseeing their every reading. None looked at the prisoner, but DuBois could see that they were all wearing the metal skullcaps.

But that was not what truly caused DuBois' mouth to go agape. No, that was left for what waited for him in the bridge's very center. For there it was that he saw either the most ludicrous, or most sinister, personage he had ever met in his life.

Seated in a great metal chair, almost a throne in size and shape, rested a figure clad in a scarlet-red satin monk's robe, hood over his face. From head to foot the voluminous folds enveloped the figure, with the exception of similarly-tinted gloves over his long tapered hands and slippers upon his feet. Upon the chest of the robe, sewn there with a border of silver thread, a stylized image of a huge spider stared back at him, its many evil red eyes represented by tiny rubies. Unlike the rest of the robe, its body was a deep, velvety chocolate in shade.

But it was the figure's eyes that caught and arrested DuBois. Hidden deep within the black oval of the hood, they glittered out upon him with a malevolence that could not be disguised. Small, gray, knife-like in sharpness; they were the eyes of both genius and madman. DuBois instantly knew he was in the presence of a killer.

"Wh-who are you?"

"You may call me The Brown Recluse," came the silky reply.

"What do you want? What is the meaning of this?"

The man calling himself The Brown Recluse leaned back in his "throne" and seemed to regard his prisoner with a great deal of amusement. "You are Dr. Emmanuel DuBois, current member of The Omega Group, a private scientific research establishment."

"Yes. Yes, I am. And?"

"Currently, you and your colleagues are working on a device you refer to as a Marconi Field Intensifier."

DuBois' face paled. "How could you know that?"

"I have my methods, Doctor. I have my methods. The reason you are being held here is this—I want this device. Or rather, I want the part of it you can give me."

"Who *are* you?"

From somewhere within the folds of his hood, The Recluse smiled. "I am a man with a mission, Doctor. A mission to save this sorry world from itself. Look outside your window sometime. Tell me, what do you see? Eh? I shall tell you. Chaos, incompetence, foolishness, superstition, lazy and idle men. *Waste.* A world going to hell in a hand basket, because it is too stupid to govern itself properly. And who governs? Imbeciles. Career politicians, tin pot dictators, religious fanatics, and, worst of all, the vulgar, uneducated rabble this country calls a *democracy.* I call them fools! It is time for this world to come under a new philosophy, Doctor, a new means of controlling production and human endeavor that is *truly* efficient. I mean the rule of those who are actually educated in the Twin Pillars of Logic and Reason. I mean the *Scientist*."

DuBois cocked his head. "You mean *technocracy*? The movement that was briefly popular a few years back? Ergs and all that? What nonsense! I'm a scientist and even I know that would never work! You mean to tell me you're a true believer in a dead cause?"

Slowly The Recluse stood before his captive, eyes snapping furiously. "Technocracy is hardly 'dead,' Doctor DuBois. I intend not only to revive it as a viable system; I intend to force the world to its views! I am spinning a great web, a Web of Tomorrow, and your invention is going to help me finish it!"

"You're mad!" Even though still held firmly, DuBois tried to lunge at his captor. To his complete surprise, The Recluse suddenly staggered back. "No! Do not try to touch me! Slaves, hold the prisoner!"

In response the two zombies squeezed DuBois's arms so hard he had to stop struggling. It was not until he had stopped struggling that The Recluse visibly relaxed. "Now. As I was saying, I know full well about your invention. And I know that, with just a little more…shall we say, 'application'—what it is capable of doing. That is why it must be mine."

"Then make one yourself!"

The Brown Recluse chortled. "My dear Dr. DuBois," he said. "I already have." A gloved hand pointed to a far corner.

DuBois had no choice but to follow the finger, and gasped at what he saw. There, standing on a concrete base supporting its weight, rested what looked for all the world like some kind of cannon. But such a cannon! It was as tall as the ceiling of the bridge. Instead of the smooth surface of the real weapon, every inch was covered—nay, *buried*—beneath a mishmashed labyrinth of wires, coils, gears and dials, all somehow merging together some contraption out of a collaboration between Verne and Lovecraft. Oddly, the "barrel" of the cannon was pointing downward, straight toward the bridge's deck. DuBois wondered why that was.

"As you can see, Doctor, I have already constructed my own version of the Marconi Field Intensifier! Albeit in this case, one much larger than your prototype. It needs to be, for my use."

"H-how did you ever get the plans?"

"You shall learn momentarily. For now, suffice to say the actual construction of the device was relatively simple. But its application—that is another story. After all, you and your colleagues designed it to only work when certain very complex algorithms are computed into its calculating machine. Algorithms so complex, in fact, that no one man can memorize them all. So you in The Omega Group devised an ingenious plan. You simply divided the algorithms between yourselves. Some trusted theirs to paper; others were able to commit theirs to memory. You did the latter."

DuBois' eyes were wide. "H-how can you know all this?"

The Brown Recluse extended an arm. "Through the help of my second-in-command," he said as another figure stepped from the shadows. A slender man, somewhere in his thirties, with sandy hair and a pencil-thin mustache.

"Horworth! My God! But you're—you're one of us! How can you turn against us like this?"

Horworth shrugged. "For money and power, DuBois, what else? The Recluse here made me an offer I couldn't refuse."

"And that is not the end of the surprises," laughed The Recluse, and suddenly drew back his hood. DuBois screamed.

"Great Heaven Above! Not you!" He looked around wildly. "I know why you wanted me now! You need my algorithms! You won't get them! I'll never tell!"

Horworth sighed. "DuBois, you already have. All we had to do was put *this* on you." He held up a metal skullcap. The zombie helmet.

"Indeed!" chuckled The Recluse. "With the cap on, you had no choice but to tell us all we wanted to know. The algorithm is already in the calculating machine! And so we no longer need *you*!" He pointed back to the device. "You see the barrel pointing toward the floor, DuBois? I need it facing downwards for a reason. But, to avoid it destroying my deck…" He flipped a switch upon his armrest. Next to the contraption, two panels retracted away from the floor, leaving only a gaping maw of blue sky beneath.

"Drop him through," The robed man instructed his zombies.

"No! No! Horworth, do something! Please! My God! *Nooooooo…..*" The scream was cut off as the panels closed.

"Well, that was fun," said Horworth dryly. "Now what?"

The Recluse leaned back in his throne. "Now we return to the Omega Group, Horworth," he answered calmly, as if he hadn't just condemned a man to a hideous death. "It seems Macek is going to bring us a guest. It would be impolite not to meet him when he gets there."

The white-haired man climbed out of the taxi, paid, and paused to look around. Nearly beneath the shadow of the famous Empire State Building, the little neighborhood of turn-of-the-century brownstones seemed quiet and genteel.

With a sigh the man glanced upwards to the towering skyscraper and thought this might be something the gentleman there might well be intrigued by. But that particular doctor was out of town. And there was no way he was involving that hotel owner he had heard of. That character's temper was legendary, and the fellow didn't even wear a shirt half the time. No, there was only one person he could trust implicitly to deal with this matter, and he was right here in this neighborhood.

The man began to walk down the street. A few of the local kids gave him curious looks. With his thick shock of white hair, elegantly clipped frosty mustache, and clad in a suit fashionable only about thirty years ago, the arrival cut a most eccentric figure.

A paperboy came along, hawking the day's copy of *The Clarion:* "*Wuxtry! Wuxtry! Read all about it! Body found on top of tree in Jersey Barrens! Corpse found tangled in highest branches! Police at a loss to explain! Wuxtry!* Paper, mister?"

The man took one and handed the boy a dime. As he scanned the headlines, a sad look crossed his face. Then he took a deep breath, steeled himself, and marched straight toward one particular edifice.

It was a small but well-kept brownstone about two stories high, with a black and inconspicuous, but nonetheless expensive, coupe parked right outside. The man climbed the short flight to the front door and noted a square brass plaque screwed into the wall. It read, in plain letters: K. HARDY

Swallowing a bit—after all, it had been fifteen years—the elderly man pressed the doorbell and waited.

An intercom speaker was inserted next to the bell. In a moment, a feminine voice emitted from it. The words were polite, but the accent was purest Flatbush:

"Kent Hardy's office. How can I help you?"

"I would like to speak to Mr. Hardy." The voice was dignified, carrying with it a very posh English accent.

"Do you have an appointment?"

"No. But tell him Professor Anton Macek wishes to see him. It's very important."

"Just a moment and I'll see if he's available."

With his jet-black hair and square jaw some said Kent Hardy resembled a certain famous cop from Chicago. Others compared him to a little known actor named Ralph Byrd. Regardless of who resembled him the most, of one thing there was no doubt—Kent Hardy was one of the best freelance criminologists in New York City.

Admittedly he was not as famous as some. Several others, such as Hammond and Noel, had much greater public reputations. But that was because Hardy liked it that way. He had never much cared for the spotlight, preferring to keep most of his investigations under his hat. Yet, all unknown to the general public, Kent Hardy had under his belt the solutions to some of the most puzzling crimes the city had ever known, from the Hallworth Murders to the Bleek Street Strangler. For those in the know, Hardy was the one you went to when you had a most bizarre case that you needed solved quickly, efficiently...and discreetly.

That knowledge had been enough for Hardy not only to make a living, but to have quietly earned himself enough to have bought the entire brownstone and made it his own. Within its walls he had created for himself a massive filing system containing the records of every known criminal in the tri-state area, a thorough library of volumes covering every topic in law, criminology, and science he felt he might need, and a small but complete crime lab in the basement he used to examine clues he discovered in the course of his cases. "What can I say?" Hardy would smile whenever asked about it. "It's a living."

"Hey, Boss?"

At the Flatbush voice Hardy looked up from his paperwork. "Yes, Dizzy?"

An odd name to call one's secretary, but Delores Baines had been known as "Dizzy" all her life. It was the only moniker that seemed to fit. Tall and gangly, rather like a stretched-out paper doll, Dizzy Baines had a mane of unruly ginger hair that never seemed in place and a visage that, while hardly ugly, could only be called "pleasantly horse-faced." A scatterbrained aura seemed to cling to her, and it had to be admitted she often seemed clueless about the simplest things. But she was just about the only secretary Hardy could find that would take all the odd hours and things he made her do, so she had been with him for the past six years.

She was also obviously in love with him. But there was nothing he could do about that.

"Visitor, Boss. Name was May-sek or something. Wanted to see you."

"Macek? You don't mean Professor Anton Macek of Yale?" Hardy nearly leapt out of his chair. "For goodness' sakes, Dizzy, let him in! My god, it's been *years*. I—but wait a moment!"

As Dizzy watched, her boss reached into his desk drawer and removed a canister of hair pomade. The label read: "Fancy Sam's Gentlemen's Hair Gloss." With deft fingers he swept up a daub and ran it over his scalp. Then, taking out a comb, he made sure that every stray follicle was slick and in its place.

Kent Hardy was not a vain man, but he possessed one major conceit. His hair had to be immaculate at all times.

Then, calling for Dizzy to bring coffee, he went to meet his visitor.

"Professor Macek!" Hardy cried, grasping the old man's hands and shaking vigorously. "How wonderful to see you again!"

The smile on the Professor's face was genuine. "Kent, my boy. It's good to see you, too."

"Dizzy," Hardy explained as his secretary entered carting a steaming mug and two cups, "This is Anton Macek, my science professor back at Yale. The smartest man I ever met and the kindest. Professor, my secretary, Delores Baines."

"How do," Dizzy said politely.

"Miss Baines," the Professor gallantly bowed with a slight kiss of her hand. At the action the secretary blushed. Forcing a semi-curtsey, she turned to her boss and arched an eyebrow as if to say, "*And why don't you ever do this?*"

Hardy changed the subject, fast. "So what brings you here, Professor? What can I help you with?"

A dark shadow flickered across his old mentor's face. "Well, my boy, I may have a case for you. Something has…happened. Would you, by chance, have seen a copy of this morning's *Clarion*?"

Hardy nodded. "Odd front page story. The body of a man was found horribly mangled in the Jersey Barrens—entwined in the branches of a tree. From the injuries, experts think that it must have not have been put up into the tree, but literally fallen into it—from a very great height. The body has not been identified yet."

"It shall not. Not for a while. But I can tell you who it is. That corpse is all that remains of Doctor Emmanuel DuBois, a brilliant researcher in the field of radio."

Now it was Hardy's eyebrow that arched. "Have a seat, Professor."

With a long sigh and heavy face, Professor Macek lowered his coffee cup. "Since you last saw me, Kent, I left Yale to go into the private sector. For the past several years I have been working with an independent research laboratory called the Omega Group. Our specialty is research into the function and uses of radio waves."

"I've heard of it. Go on."

"We are a small organization—only six members. But I trust I am not bragging when I state that nonetheless there is more genius in our facility than in most universities today. We are all what you might term 'Renaissance Scientists'—interested and studying in just about every branch. Radio simply happens to be our main interest at the moment."

"I love radio, myself," Dizzy put in. "*Amos and Andy* is my favorite program."

Before her employer could say anything, Macek came to the rescue. "Well, our research really isn't along those lines, my dear," he smiled. "We are far more interested in the actual application of radio waves for use as a potential power source rather than just a medium for spreading sound. Its possible function as a means for detecting the approach of airplanes in the sky, for example."

Dizzy shook her head. "Detecting things in the air? Can't picture it."

"Just a possibility, my dear. It may never happen."

"Nevertheless, you have made discoveries," Hardy encouraged.

"Yes. And advanced the field by more than twenty years, is my guess. But I'm getting ahead of myself. As I said, there are six of us—myself, Dr. DuBois, Doctor Lemuel Grimes, Doctor Jack Seeton, Doctor Benjamin Horworth, and Doctor Emil Janus. Three days ago, Dr. DuBois failed to report for work. At first we thought he was merely ill—but then we learned he had not been seen at all in all that time. His apartment was deserted and unslept in. Last night, his body was discovered. That is when we found the film."

"Film?"

"Yes. It…" Macek's voice trailed off. He rubbed his forehead. "I'm afraid the only way to show you is to show you. Will you come with me to our laboratory, Kent? It's out on Long Island—not far at all. Once there, I'm sure you'll see why…well, why I want *you* involved."

Kent Hardy leaned back in his chair thoughtfully, hands folded, fingertips resting upon his lips. Then with a fluid movement he was on his feet and reaching for his hat. "Get your coat, Dizzy," he ordered. "We're going for a little drive."

Snow was on the ground and the air was chill, but the roads were clear of hazards as Hardy's coupe navigated the back ways of Long Island. Professor Macek directed their course from next to Hardy, while Dizzy sat in the back—delivering adoring glances toward her boss when she thought he wasn't looking.

"No, my boy," the Professor was saying. "My colleagues won't hear of contacting the police. What this madman wants is—well, you'll see. And what you'll see will astonish you. There's our laboratory now."

He pointed as the coupe approached a chain-link fence surrounding a snow-covered field. A few hundred yards from the gate, a long, low pale building of peeling whitewash and small, cramped windows was waiting for them. It looked like a disused dairy building, which is indeed what it had been. At the Professor's command, Hardy drove through the gate.

"Doesn't look very promising," Dizzy murmured under her breath as she climbed out.

Macek heard. "Oh, but wait until you get inside. Now come and meet my colleagues."

With a glow of pride he ushered them through the small wooden door that served as an entrance. Once inside, even Dizzy had to admit she was impressed.

The cavernous interior of the building had been completely refurbished. Where once was a mass of stables holding cows and milking machines was now a gleaming research establishment modern in every detail. Soft arc lighting provided perfect illumination to every corner. Here were polished laboratory benches replete with every tool known to man; in organized cabinets running clear across the wall rested every sort of instrumentation and device needed for the growing science of radio. No, Dizzy thought, they didn't mess around with *Amos and Andy* here. The investigations of the Omega Group was far more advanced than that.

In the center of the room, obviously waiting for them, waited a group of four white-coated men. Macek came forward.

"Gentlemen, let me introduce to you Kent Hardy—the man I feel certain is going to help us out of our predicament. And Miss Baines, his secretary."

Rather than saying anything, the four looked dubiously upon the newcomers. Hardy mentally identified each from the descriptions Macek had given him on the way:

There was Seeton, fiftyish and completely bald. After a minute, he reluctantly stuck out his hand in greeting. Grimes, tall and cadaverous with the pan of a depressed mule, regarded the criminologist with glum grey

*At the Professor's command, Hardy drove through the gate.*

eyes. Horworth, a slender fellow somewhere in his thirties with sandy hair and a pencil-thin mustache, seemed pleased to see hello, shaking his hand in a firm, steady grip. Lastly, Emil Janus bowed graciously but made no move to shake hands. He was a fair-sized gentleman with a regal, aquiline nose and a high intellectual forehead. A pencil-thin mustache as elegant as Macek's graced his upper lip and clear, intelligent blue eyes gazed out intently at him. "Please forgive my manners," he said apologetically, "but I never shake hands."

Grimes spoke up immediately thereafter. "Look here, Macek," he said, "I don't see why we need to bring a private detective into this fiasco. Just what do you think he can accomplish? If this 'Brown Recluse' is telling the truth, he can kill any one of us as easily as he killed DuBois. I say we hand over the algorithms! Give him what he wants!"

"Don't be a fool!" Seeton snapped. "You know as well as anyone what the Intensifier can do! How can we put that sort of power into anyone's hands? Do you want the blood of potentially millions on your hands? Because I don't!"

"Gentlemen, gentlemen, please!" Macek threw up his hands. "Let's not argue with each other! Poor DuBois is dead! We cannot help him now! But we can help ourselves, and perhaps all those others you speak of, Seeton! But, to do that we need Hardy!" He wheeled toward his two other partners. "Don't you agree?" he asked pleadingly.

Taking a deep breath, Janus exhaled uncertainly. "I must admit this goes against my better judgment, Macek. What we have here is potentially very dangerous, indeed. But I am forced to agree that we must do something. If you think this Mr. Hardy can help us, then I trust your judgment. Horworth?"

The younger man nodded. "I say let's see what he can do."

"Thank you, gentlemen," Macek said, smiling in relief. "I assure you, Hardy is both efficient and discreet. If anyone can get to the bottom of this, it is he."

"And thank you for the vote of confidence, Professor," Hardy replied, but his face was serious. "But if I *am* to help you, then obviously I need to know what's going on. Now, I know that several days ago one of your colleagues vanished and was just yesterday found dead—hanging from the top of a tree. And you said you received a film of some kind the very night he was found. Do you still have this film?"

"We do," replied Seeton.

"And may I see this film?"

Four heads turned toward Grimes. He frowned. Four pairs of eyes continued to bore into him. He sighed, said, "If you must," and motioned for everyone to follow.

Within moments they found themselves in a little side room, where a loaded film projector rested, waiting upon a table. A screen had already been set up. "Watch," Grimes ordered and flipped the lights. With the hum of the motor the projector started. A second later and upon the screen flickered the appearance of man. A man whose face was lost within the folds of a monk's hood, but whose glittering eyes could be seen glaring like malevolent icicles even on the flat dimensions of the screen.

"Men of the Omega Group," the figure said in a cold voice. "I am the Brown Recluse."

"Brown Recluse?" hissed Dizzy. "What's a Brown Recluse?"

"A venomous spider from the American South and Midwest," Hardy whispered back. "Now stop interrupting!"

The voice of The Recluse droned on. "By the time this film is delivered to you, you shall have learned of the peculiar demise of your associate, Dr. Emmanuel DuBois. I arranged that demise. I did so to show you that I am serious in my demands of you, and that I intend for them to be met."

Eyes glimmered furiously upon the screen. "I shall not mince words. Even as we speak, your organization is experimenting with a device you call the Marconi Field Intensifier. This device requires the use of several complex algorithms placed within its calculating machine in order for it to function. Because these algorithms are too complex for any one man to memorize completely, you have each chosen to either memorize, or write down, a partial set individually. You shall deliver these algorithms to me. If you do not, each one of you shall meet the same fate as the misfortunate Dr. DuBois. I do not joke about this. Give the algorithms to me. I shall inform you of the manner in which they are to be delivered at a later date. That is all."

With that, the end of the film flopped within the reel. Grimes shut off the projector and turned on the lights.

Hardy was leaning forward, fingertips pressed thoughtfully upon his lips. "The Brown Recluse…" Then he glanced toward the Professor. "What is a Marconi Field Intensifier?"

"We'll show you," the Professor said.

It was the weirdest looking thing Dizzy had ever seen. Resting atop a laboratory bench, it resembled nothing so much as a foot tall, two foot long metal cannon. But a cannon covered from top to toe with such an incredible array of wires, coils, gauges and dials that the original surface of the thing couldn't be seen.

"This is a working prototype we constructed," Seeton said. "Our only prototype, in fact. We've been experimenting with it for the past several months."

"What does it do?" Dizzy asked.

Janus rubbed his chin. "With all due respect, I'm not certain you'd understand the technical aspects of it, Miss Baines," he apologized. "But in layman's terms we are trying to develop a device that can emit, if you will, solid radio transmissions."

"*Solid* radio transmissions?" Hardy said incredulously.

"Well, perhaps that's a bit of a misnomer," Horworth put in. "A better way to put it might be that we're developing radio waves that can actually create a physical effect upon the environment. Here, let me demonstrate. Grimes, put that concrete block on the bench, will you? Thanks."

Horworth's fingers flew over a series of switches along the "cannon." As they did, its wires and coils began humming. Dials flickered. A shrill, sharp-pitched whine began to fill the air, causing their ears to ring. "Now watch!" Grimes cried loudly over the whine, and taking the device aimed the "nose" of the "cannon" right at the concrete block.

The whine grew even more high-pitched. Before the cannon it seemed as if the air began to shimmer and wave. As the machine called the Intensifier continued, the concrete block started to tremble. Then quiver. As they watched, cracks began to appear along its hard surface. Tiny bits of gravel dropped from its sides. Then, just as the Intensifier reached its highest pitch, the block exploded before their very eyes!

Even as it did, the wheels and gears of the Intensifier started sparking. Immediately Horworth shut the machine down, flapping the sparks away with the hem of his jacket. "It must be that inducer coil again," he said, pointing to a particular spiraling piece of metal. "Every time that goes, the whole thing shorts out."

"Wow!" Dizzy pounded her ears with the palm of her hand. "My ears haven't rung like that since the morning after I graduated high school." She paused as she saw everyone staring at her. "Uh…well, you see, things got pretty wild that night…"

"Thank you, Dizzy," Hardy cut her off drily. "Now I think I understand what you were talking about, Professor."

"Yes, my boy. While this is just a prototype, you can see the power of the Intensifier. So imagine what it could do if someone constructed a larger version. Homes, businesses—perhaps entire cities—could be destroyed. That's why we have never released news of this to the public. And that's why we do not want the police involved in this."

"This Brown Recluse found out about it, just the same," Hardy murmured, almost half to himself. "I wonder...well, not just now. All right. So, The Recluse wants the algorithms needed to properly use this device, eh? And each of you has part of them? On paper, or in your head?"

"DuBois had his in his head," Macek said. "As do I."

"On paper," Horworth said.

"On paper," Seeton said.

"On paper," Grimes said sourly.

"On paper and in my head," Janus finished.

"Very well. Gentlemen, I do believe you're going to need my help after all. I accept your case."

"Great!" Horworth exclaimed. "What are you going to do?"

"First, go back to my office and start checking my sources for anything on this Brown Recluse. We'll see from there."

"And us?" queried Janus. "What should we do in the meantime?"

"Truthfully, gentlemen? Be careful! Be very careful! Come on, Dizzy, let's head back to the office...."

Several hours later, Dr. Grimes rested upon a chair in his small home, trying to read the paper.

There were many things Lemuel Grimes did not like. Children. Animals. Just about everything else. But most of all, he hated interruptions and company.

So his face was even more sour than normal when he answered the knock upon the door.

"Oh," he said when he saw his visitor, "It's you. Well, I suppose you can come in."

As he stepped back to let his guest inside, he glanced down suspiciously at the parcel beneath the other's arm. "What's that?"

"A box."

"I *know* it's a box. What's in it?"

"Just a little something I thought you could use."

Grimes snorted. "I don't need anything—save perhaps that idiot detective doing something actually useful! What was Macek thinking when he brought that young man in? He barely looks intelligent enough to get a cat out of a tree. Personally, I think we shou—what are you doing? Why are you opening that box? What on earth is that—some kind of colander? Here! Stop! Don't put that thing on me! What in heaven's name do you think you are..."

As the metallic skullcap came over his head, Grimes' body jerked like an electric current had been turned on inside. His face slackened even its perpetual disdainfulness. His eyes grew blank and locked straight ahead.

"Lemuel Grimes," his guest said softly, "You are now under the power of The Brown Recluse. You will get your algorithms for me."

Like a moving corpse, the body of Grimes turned and stepped flatly toward his fireplace. Right above the mantel there rested a painting showing a restful rustic scene. Grimes swing this painting outward toward himself.

Resting within the wall was the iron door of a safe. Grimes reached stiff fingers out and manipulated the lock. With a groan the door slowly pulled open. From within, Grimes withdrew a small sheath of papers. These he handed wordlessly and mindlessly to his guest.

"Thank you, Grimes," The Brown Recluse said. "Now why don' t you come with me? I'm going out of town for the night, and I would just *love* to drop you off somewhere."

Upon the bridge of *The Spider's Eye*, The Brown Recluse reclined in his throne, surveying his kingdom. It was a small kingdom, to be sure. Just a bridge in a zeppelin. But soon, very soon now, it would grow. Grow faster and farther than the world could ever dream possible.

And it was an efficient kingdom. Everywhere his glittering eyes looked, his subjects moved and worked with the inhuman precision of worker ants. No unneeded motions were wasted. No unnecessary thoughts or emotions distracted his Maton-Men from their duties. He had made it so. Through his mind control helmets, The Brown Recluse had created the perfect laborer.

He had gathered them all from various places. Bread lines, soup kitchens, Hoovervilles. The more intelligent ones he placed in maintaining the engines of *The Spider's Eye* or upon certain projects he was working on. The others he set to doing manual labor in other parts of the ship. He rather regarded it as a public service. After all, what would these men be doing otherwise without him? Nothing; lying around idly, lazily, producing nothing of use. In the new world, the world of his Web of Tomorrow, there would be no such layabouts. He would see to it.

It had taken him years to reach this point. Years of secretly offering his inventions, his genius, to various criminal enterprises in exchange for outrageous sums of money. Years of subordinating himself to idiots in order to fund this, his ultimate goal. But now the seeds of his labors were about to bear fruit. If Macek's pet could be prevented from interfering...

Coming to a decision, he rose from his chair and moved across the bridge to where an advanced radio set awaited. He set it to a certain frequency and lifted the microphone. "B-R 1 to H," he intoned. "B-R 1 to H."

A brief sea of static, then a voice from across the either. Horworth's voice. "H to B-R 1. Go ahead."

"Now that we have Mr. Hardy as a new piece on the game board, I feel we are going to have to remove him from it. Pick a likely candidate to process his elimination. It doesn't matter who."

"No problem, boss. And Macek?"

"I will deal with him at the proper time. Your job is to simply follow orders. And my orders are, kill Hardy!"

🌺 🌺 🌺

"All right, Mike, thanks." With a frustrated expression on his face, Kent Hardy replaced the receiver atop his phone.

Thus far, all his inquiries were proving fruitless. He had contacted all his various underworld sources, from drug-addled stool pigeons to high-up mobsters, for any information they could give on the personage calling himself The Brown Recluse. Each time, he received the same answer. Vague mutterings of a red-robed man offering advanced scientific knowledge and equipment to certain criminals over the years. Then, like the spider whose name he bore, the figure would scuttle back into the shadows, never coming forward on his own. Whomever The Recluse was, he kept his head down.

Well, that had apparently changed, Hardy mused. But what was his purpose? His motives? He wanted the algorithms necessary to power the

Marconi Field Intensifier, true. And yet—The Recluse had not demanded the construction blueprints for the actual *invention*. Why hadn't he? What good were the algorithms without that?

And how had he even known about the Omega Group's experiments in the first place? An idea was forming in Hardy's mind, and he didn't like what it meant.

"Boss?"

He looked up to find Dizzy hovering concernedly over him. "Are you still here? It's late, Dizzy—go on home."

His secretary snorted. "Go home? I just came in to work! Boss, it's six-thirty in the *morning*. You've been researching all night!"

"Oh."

"You probably haven't eaten a thing. I'm going to get some blueberry blintzes. My sainted mother always said—"

"Sainted mother? Dizzy, you're Jewish."

"My sainted Jewish mother always said there's nothing like blueberry blintzes when you've been up all night. Now stay here." Grabbing her coat, she made for the front door.

She never saw the man standing right outside until she almost collided with him.

He had a face that seemed absolutely frozen. No emotion showed upon it. His eyes were glazed and locked forward. His scalp was completely covered by a metal skullcap. And he punched Dizzy right in the face.

She fell with a cry. Even as she hit the floor, the man with the frozen face slammed a foot unheedingly upon her chest, sending a heel deep with her stomach as he stepped right over her.

At the sound of the cry Hardy stepped into the hallway: "Dizzy?" He stopped as he saw the man with the frozen face—a man otherwise quite ordinary in appearance—step cruelly across his secretary. The man's blank eyes met his.

"KENT—HARDY—MUST—DIE!" the man with the frozen face roared, and charged.

Instantly Hardy dived back into the interior of his office, reaching for the 1911 A1 45 Caliber he had left within its holster. The man with the frozen face slammed into his back, knocking him to the carpet. The man's hands clutched wildly, inexorably for Hardy's throat. And yet his face showed not one sign of joy or fury. It remained flat and tight as a store mannequin's face even as his voice rang out loudly but with no emotion:

"KENT—HARDY—MUST—DIE!"

Hardy pounded a fist into the man's face. He felt a crunch as the cartilage of the nose broke and a spurt of blood fell upon his knuckles. Yet the grip around his throat slackened not in the slightest. Hardy threw out his arm, straining to grab the holster hanging just inches away upon the back of his chair. Yet the leather straps stayed tauntingly out of reach. Hardy's adam's apple felt about to collapse. Stars flashed before his eyes…

"*KENT!*"

From nowhere came a woman's voice with a thick Flatbush accent, then a metallic *clunk!* Immediately the fingers ceased their steel-like grip. The man with the frozen face drew back, shivering wildly, as if an electrical charge had just vibrated throughout his body. Then he collapsed forward, blood streaming from his broken nose, revealing a bare head of ordinary brown hair. "Oohhhhh…." he moaned.

Hardy forced his head to stop swimming. Once more he saw Dizzy standing over him. This time she was holding the odd metallic skullcap in her hands. As soon as the man had slammed into Kent, she had forced herself to her feet. Racing to save her boss, she snatched at the first thing she saw—the bowl-like cap covering the man's head. Yanking it up, she promptly turned it over and sent it crashing down upon their attacker.

Still gasping for air, Hardy struggled to his feet. Dizzy helped him up, trying and failing to hide the concern she felt. "Are you all right?"

"I'll be fine in a minute, Dizzy," Hardy assured her. "Now who's our guest here?"

The man with the frozen face rolled over on his back. And now they saw that his face was no longer so frozen. In fact, it was quite twisted, with pain and confusion. "Wha—what happened?" The man finally spluttered out, clutching at his injured nose. "Where am I? Who the hell are you?"

"Who the hell are *you?*" Hardy snapped. "And what do you mean bursting into my office, assaulting my secretary, and trying to kill me?"

"Wha? What are you talking about, buddy? My name's Jack Taylor—I'm a street cleaner! I was getting ready for work when some guy came up behind me and slammed something on my head. Next thing I know I'm here with a bloody nose! What's going on?" The man calling himself Jack Taylor looked up at them with an expression so confused the criminologist strangely found himself believing him.

"Was this the 'thing?'" he asked, taking the skullcap from Dizzy.

"I—I guess so. It all happened so fast. What is that thing, mister?"

Hardy peered at the metal colander-like object intently. "That's rather what I'd like to know myself," he said at last. "Fetch the first aid kit, Dizzy.

*From nowhere came a metallic clunk!*

And then call Professor Macek and ask him if he can come over. I'd rather like him to see something."

"Extraordinary, my boy." The surface of the skullcap glinted in the light as Macek held it high. "Most extraordinary! Look at the wiring in the interior! Most compact!"

With a flip, he revealed the inside of the helmet. Crisscrossed within was a mass of multi-colored wires arranged in a fashion that seemed far too many, and far too awkward, than to fit inside. "And you said that this man who attacked you was wearing this at the time?"

"Yes." After a period of intensive questioning, Hardy had satisfied himself that the unfortunate Jack Taylor indeed knew nothing about what had occurred prior to having "some mug" slap the helmet now in Macek's possession upon his head. Efforts to get a decent description had failed: "I didn't get a good gander at him, mister." At a loss on what to do next, they had patched up his nose, handed him a hundred dollar bill in exchange for a promise to let the matter drop, and sent him on his way.

"Odd, very odd! I wonder what it is for?"

Hardy met his old mentor's eyes seriously. "I have a possibility. Professor, what are the chances a radio transmitter could be invented that could actually take over a human mind?"

"Take over a—hmm. Well…I can't say it's absolutely impossible, my boy. After all, the human brain is operated by a series of electrical impulses. Theoretically, it could be *possible* for a series of radio waves, very specially calibrated, to overwhelm and 'short-circuit' brainwaves. In fact, very early on, the Group was interested in such an idea. But we abandoned it on moral grounds."

"I see. Thank you, Professor. Now, I—"

Dizzy suddenly stuck her head in. "Professor Macek! Dr. Janus is on the line!"

"Yes, I told the others I'd be here. Well, except Grimes; he didn't answer his phone. What does he want?"

"He's in a panic! His home was robbed last night! The algorithms he had were stolen!"

Dr. Emil Janus was pale and drawn. "I can't believe it! My own house, robbed!"

Kent Hardy and Professor Macek were looking at the wide open door of a small safe tucked away in an obscure closet. Hardy was going over it with a magnifying glass.

"I was feeling tense from all this madness, so I decided to go out for dinner! When I came home, I found the door open and my safe rifled! They took the algorithms and nothing else!"

"Now, now, Emil," Macek said soothingly. "Try not to worry. At least you weren't here when it happened and are unharmed!" He reached out, as if to place a hand on his partner's shoulder, but, remembering, drew it away at the last moment.

With a grunt Hardy pocketed his glass and stood. "No good here," he said. "No fingerprints at all. Didn't expect any, really, but worth a try."

"Hardy—" Janus' voice was low. "Do you really think you can catch this madman?"

Hardy looked at him soberly. "I cannot promise to be successful, Doctor. But I can promise to do everything in my power to find The Brown Recluse and bring him to justice."

"Then that shall be enough."

"Thank you. May I use your phone? I need to check in at my office."

"Of course."

"Thanks. Operator, TREmont-5555, please. Hello, Dizzy? Kent. I—what's that? What? I see. Yes. Right. Goodbye."

Slowly Hardy replaced the receiver. His face was grim.

"What's wrong, my boy?"

"A mounted policeman in Central Park found the remains of a mangled body trapped in the upper branches of a tree. It has been identified positively as the body of Lemuel Grimes. A search of his home by the police found his safe wide open."

Macek's eyes went wide. "Grimes...is dead?"

"I'm afraid so."

With infinite weariness Janus flopped down upon his sofa and rubbed his eyes. "Good Lord. What will this madman do next? He's already killed two of us and stolen their algorithms!"

"He may have more than that," muttered Hardy.

Macek blinked. "What do you mean, my boy?"

Kent Hardy took a deep breath. He knew his mentor was not going to like what he had to say next. "It is my belief that The Brown Recluse is none other than a member of the Omega Group itself."

"*WHAT??*" Macek's eyes went wide. Janus' mouth dropped open, appalled.

"Hear me out. It is obvious The Recluse wants to build his own version of the Marconi Field Intensifier—otherwise, why would he want the algorithms for it? But the algorithms are useless without the machine itself. Yet not once has The Brown Recluse demanded the plans for the actual construction of the Intensifier. That can only mean one thing—The Recluse *already has* the plans to build one; perhaps already *has* built it. Where did he get them from? He must have gotten them from the lab; there's no other explanation. Therefore, one of the Group either must be The Recluse, or must have given it to him.

"Second. The unfortunate man who attacked Dizzy and I was being controlled by the helmet he was wearing. This 'zombie cap,' so to speak, was powered by a special type of radio wave capable of controlling the brain waves of an individual. Professor Macek has already told me the Group at one point had been looking into such research, but had abandoned it. Yet there the helmet was. Once again, there's only one logical explanation—someone in the Group did *not* abandon the research, but continued it in secret. And he perfected it."

"This is a serious charge, my boy!" Macek declared fiercely. "And yet—I have to admit, it fits the facts of the case so far."

"Nonsense!" declaimed Janus. "Hardy is—"

"No, Emil. As much as I hate to admit it, Kent is right. One of us must be The Brown Recluse. And he is killing us one by one."

"Yes," nodded Hardy. "DuBois memorized his algorithm, but Grimes had his on paper. Therefore, all The Recluse needed to do was steal it if that is all he wanted. But he chose to kill Grimes, anyway. He wishes the rest of the Omega Group dead. Probably to prevent a rival Intensifier from being built."

"But I wasn't murdered," Janus protested. "I was only robbed."

"Which means nothing. You were simply not here when The Recluse struck. Your life could still be in danger."

"Then I must leave town at once!" Janus sprang to his feet. "I'm not going to stay here while some madman hunts me down! I'm leaving at once! Anton, come with me!"

"I don't recommend that," Hardy replied. "You need police protection. I can—"

"No! The police can do nothing! I'm going! If you are fool enough not to come, Anton, then all I can wish you is good luck! But I'm leaving!" Before

Hardy could stop him he was out of the room.

Macek put a hand on his student's shoulder. "Let him go, my boy. We can serve him best by stopping The Recluse."

From outside they could hear the loud engine of Janus's little car start, then from the window they saw it pass, a figure at the wheel. Then the windows rattled and the two men were knocked to the floor by the force of the blast.

Emil Janus' car had exploded with him inside!

Horworth hated being near the Maton-Men. Their living dead faces and toy soldier movements gave him the creeps. But his boss had given order that he be escorted by one at all times while aboard *The Spider's Eye*. So he tolerated the presence of the blank-eyed zombie as it walked with him through the sliding door to the bridge.

"Thanks, Frankenstein," he said as the Maton-Man immediately froze the moment it passed the threshold. "I'll take it from here."

Strictly speaking, there was a large part of him wondering why he was even "here" in the first place. When the man who was The Brown Recluse had first taken him aside in secret, telling him he sensed he, Horworth, was just the sort of man he was looking for, Horworth thought the man had lost his mind. This quiet, scholarly fellow a super-criminal? It couldn't be. Besides, Horworth was a respected member of the scientific establishment despite his youth. True, it didn't pay very much, but the principle of the matter…

But then The Recluse had shown him just what he had to offer him. Money. Women. Power. Especially power. And Benjamin Horworth threw his principles out the window. Besides, he had a sneaking feeling he might have ended up a Maton-Man himself if he had said no, and *that* wasn't going to happen.

But the boss seemed to be treating this whole thing like it was some crazy game, and he wanted it to end. The Recluse had made him promises, dammit! And he meant to have them.

Surprisingly, The Recluse was not to be found in his throne. He was standing before his large Intensifier, gently running his hands over its gauges and dials with almost erotic fascination. It made Horworth more than a little uncomfortable.

"Isn't it a beautiful thing?" The Recluse whispered as he caressed its cold steel. "A lovely, lovely pearl sent from above. Sent just for me."

Horworth snorted. "I wouldn't say just for you, Boss. Remember I had a lot to do in the designing of that thing, too."

The Recluse sighed, not turning around. "Why are you here? I did not summon you."

"Because I'm wondering when we're going to quit playing around and finish this." He stepped closer to his master. "We've already got half the algorithms—let's stop beating around the bush and get the rest. Hardy is getting closer and closer to figuring out the whole thing. I say we grab the others and get this thing going."

Like most men do, Horworth was gesturing with his hands as he said this, throwing out his arms for emphasis. As he did, however, his fingertips creased the briefest brush against the robe of The Recluse. Instantly the mastermind wheeled upon him.

*"You almost touched me!"*

Horworth drew back, realizing his mistake at once. "Whoa! Sorry! I didn't mean—"

*"Never touch me again! Ever!!!"* The Recluse's eyes were inflamed gray diamonds, burning with an infuriated fire.

"I won't! I won't!" Horworth was stepping away frantically, a look of abject fear upon his face.

With a visible effort, The Recluse calmed himself. "Get back to the Group," he hissed through grit teeth. "Call me *only* if there is new information. I will deal with Hardy in my own time, in my own way. Is that clear?"

"Yes, I—"

*"Is that clear??"*

"Yes, sir! Yes, sir!"

"Then, go," The Recluse told him, "And pray I forget what you almost did here today. If you don't want to end up like DuBois and Grimes."

Professor Anton Macek sat in the darkened room of Janus's house, shades drawn. Hardy let him mourn for a while.

The police had come, of course. Unwarranted explosions tended to attract attention. They weren't too happy when Hardy had explained matters to them, but, because he was Kent Hardy and he was already involved, they agreed to give him the free hand he needed.

Now he came back into the room. "Professor."

Macek shook his head. "Where will this end?"

Hardy sat and placed his arm about him. "Where it should," he said with a fierceness that belied his action, "With the end of The Brown Recluse! We've been on the defensive long enough. It's time we take the battle to him! I've got a plan that should bring us face-to-face with The Brown Recluse himself. Are you game, Professor?"

"You know better than to ask, my boy."

Hardy rewarded him with a grim smile. "Then I need you to make a call, while I get a few things in town…"

A few hours later, Kent Hardy stood before a washroom mirror. In one hand he deftly applied a last dab of Fancy Sam's onto his scalp. With the other he carefully combed it through his thick black locks until the top of his head gleamed like sunshine on ink.

"Good grief, Kent," huffed the Professor as he entered just in time to see Hardy put the last strands in place. "I know careful grooming is important, but I've never known anyone as obsessed with his hair as you. Here you are prettifying yourself when we're supposed to be setting a trap!"

Calmly Hardy smoothed back his well-oiled coiffure. "But the trap *is* set, Professor," he said enigmatically. "All we have to do now is wait for The Recluse to fall into it. Did you do everything like I asked?"

"Hmph. Yes. I called Horworth, and he said he'd let the others know. Are you sure that's what you wanted?"

"Oh, yes. We both suspect The Brown Recluse is one of the Group. And we know he wants the algorithm you have inside your head to create his own Field Intensifier. Therefore in order to bring him out, we have to force his hand. So we're going to let him get you, and me. By the end of the night, if all goes well, we should be right in the middle of the spider's den!"

"H calling B-R 1, H calling B-R 1."

"Report."

"We have a problem."

"Yes?"

"I just got a call from Macek. He says he can't take it here anymore with all the deaths. He needs to get out. So Hardy's arranged to take him to his own cabin upstate. For his own protection."

The Recluse's eyes gleamed. "Really?" He sounded almost amused.

"Yes! What are we going to do? We need that algorithm!"

"Calm yourself. Pray by chance, did Macek mention the precise route they were taking?"

"Huh? Actually, yeah he did. They're going up Old Route Ten. Why?"

The Recluse's shoulders were shaking with silent laughter. "How kind of him! How convenient! Far too convenient!"

"Huh?" Horworth asked again.

The voice of The Recluse turned serious. "Our friend Hardy means to force our hand, Horworth. He is either far more stupid, or far more intelligent, than I suspected. If he wishes to meet me so badly, I do not see a reason we should not humor him. Remember what you were saying about how it's time to 'quit playing around?' I believe you are right. It is time to quit playing. Now we must move."

"What about Seeton?"

"Take a helmet and find a way to get it on him. Then, when he has given you the algorithms, shoot him through the heart! We don't need *him*."

"All right. I'll manage. And Macek?"

"You just return to *The Spider's Eye* afterwards. You'll find out then."

Once Old Route Ten had been a major thoroughfare in the first part of this century, before newer and more modern roads had taken its traffic. Now it was a nearly deserted stretch of flat asphalt and dirt, with nary a car or truck to pass. That's why Hardy had chosen it as he directed his coupe through the night's darkness.

"Miss Baines is not with us?"

"No. She's back at the office. Too dangerous."

Macek sighed. "I just wish I knew who this madman was."

Hardy looked at him. "You mean you haven't figured it out yet?"

Macek blinked. "You mean you—"

"Oh, yes."

"Then who?" he sighed again. "Never mind. I'm sure I'll find out soon enough." The Professor craned his neck to glance through the rear window. "I don't see anyone following us."

Hardy smiled grimly. "Oh, they won't use a car or truck to get us, Professor. Remember the bodies? No, if we're attacked—*when* we're attacked—it will come from up—"

Something slammed onto the hood of the car. Something that seemed to drop from the sky.

"Above," Hardy managed to spit out as a hand came crashing through the windshield to grip the wheel of the car.

From seemingly nowhere more thuds hit the car, and clutching hands suddenly darted through the windows, clutching toward the men! It was all Hardy could do to keep control of the car. The Maton-Man who was fighting for the steering wheel kept getting in his way. In desperation Hardy slammed on the brakes and switched off the ignition.

It seemed to be what the Maton-Men were waiting for. Climbing down from hood and roof and trunk, they hauled Macek and Hardy out and held them.

"Good evening, gents!" came a voice from above.

Macek couldn't believe his eyes. It was Horworth! Horworth, hanging from a long rope ladder dangling from a huge dirigible that had lowered itself dangerously close to the ground!

"Horworth! So you're The Brown Recluse!"

The scientist laughed. "Don't you wish? No, he isn't me; just work for him. Now grab the ropes and climb up. The Brown Recluse is just dying to meet you."

"Do as he says, Professor," Hardy advised. Grimly he grasped the twine of the ladder and began climbing.

Once aboard the zeppelin, Hardy and Macek were handcuffed and shoved between the escorts of two towering Maton-Men. "Search them!" Horworth ordered. "Remove everything they could possibly use as a weapon!"

"Don't resist," Hardy warned the Professor as the thuggish slaves roughly searched their clothes. He sighed as his gun was removed, as well as wallet, shoes and belt.

That unpleasant task over, they were led, following Horworth through gleaming metal corridors where mindless zombies with metal skullcaps passed them without a second glance, to the most advanced, technical bridge either had ever seen. There, upon a regal "throne," The Brown Recluse himself waited to greet them.

The robed figure upon the throne waved his hand. "Release them." Instantly their hands were free. But the Maton-Men stayed right beside them. "Mr. Hardy. My dear Professor Macek. Welcome aboard *The Spider's Eye*. So we meet at last."

Hardy regarded the costumed figure evenly. "Oh, I wouldn't say 'at last,'" he said. "Rather, I'd say, 'again.' For we *have* met before, just recently. Haven't we?"

The Recluse leaned back and regarded the criminologist with amusement. "I'm afraid I have no idea what you mean."

"Perhaps this will help. After all, it's customary for a guest to shake his host's hand!" With lightning he pounced toward the throne. "C'mon, Recluse, shake! What are you afraid of?"

Before Macek's amazed eyes the murderer of his colleagues pulled back like he had brushed a hot stove. "*Do not touch me! Seize him!*"

"What's wrong, 'Brown Recluse?'" Hardy taunted even as he was dragged back. "Afraid to shake someone's hand? And why call yourself a Recluse? Could it be because you have a phobia of being touched–*Dr. Janus?*"

The Brown Recluse hissed with a cobra's venom. Then he slowly raised a hand to his monk's hood. The fabric pulled back. From the dark depths a small immaculate mustache appeared. An aquiline nose was revealed. Lastly, above the gleaming gray eyes, a high and intellectual forehead pulled itself into the light.

"My God!" Macek cried. "Emil! But--but we saw you die—"

"On the contrary, Professor," Hardy said. "We saw Janus' car explode. We saw a man inside. But we did not actually see if that figure was Janus."

"Too true, Mr. Hardy. That was just another piece of human flotsam, like the rest of my Maton-Men here. Formerly an apple seller, I believe. Not that it really matters. Tell me, Hardy, how did you guess it was I?"

The detective shrugged. "Not so hard, really. DuBois' and Grimes' bodies were both dropped from a great height—from this very dirigible, I should say. But you—you were different. Caught up in an explosion. Why? Because you wanted to fake your death and throw suspicion off yourself."

Janus leaned back in his throne, smiling grimly. "Very good, Mr. Hardy. It was about time for me to disappear, anyway. But I'm rather disappointed *you* didn't figure it out first, Anton. I was hoping better of you."

Macek struggled to get hold of himself. With a visible effort he looked with horror at his best friend. "Emil, what are you planning?"

The Recluse rose from his throne. Gesturing the Maton-Men to bring them, he stalked to the end of the bridge where his version of the Intensifier waited patiently.

"I *plan* the Rule of the Scientist in this world, dear Anton," he declared, indicating the great machine. "I plan the end of inefficiency and waste, and the birth of a new humanity. One purged of such weaknesses as morals and ethics, and dedicated solely to the pursuit of more knowledge. I plan the dominance of Logic and Reason."

"Under your guidance, of course," Hardy said dryly.

"Of course," The Recluse replied, unconscious of the sarcasm. "Who else has the clear mind and genius to do it but I? In the end I shall reshape poor, stupid humanity into my own image and then the golden age shall truly begin. But, regrettably, that shall take cost. There shall have to be sacrifices before the world will see the rightness of my cause. I fear I must give them a demonstration of my power."

"What are you going to do?"

The Brown Recluse smiled. "I am going to use the Intensifier to remove something I have always regarded as a mote upon the landscape. I am going to destroy New York City and everyone in it!"

"You're mad!"

"No, Anton—just practical. New York is the epicenter of the waste and inefficiency I despise. And it will serve as the demonstration I need to make the rest of the country bow before me. If it does not, I will destroy more cities, and still more, until it turns the reins of government over to me. But my Intensifier is not yet quite prepared. Are you ready to help me complete it, Anton?"

Macek snorted angrily. "Never, Emil. I could never assist you in this. Please, please, please, in the name of our old friendship, turn away from this madness. Come with us. Besides, you couldn't plug in the rest of the algorithms even if you wanted to. Seeton isn't here with his part!"

"But we don't need Seeton, Anton," Janus chuckled. From the folds of his robe he produced a sheath of papers. "Horworth has already gained for me his algorithms. Poor Seeton didn't survive the robbery, of course. Oh, well. You should feel honored, my friend, thanks to your interference, I have been forced to move my timetable up considerably. But no matter. With your help, the Intensifier shall be completed. Then I shall use it to create a massive wall of radio waves that shall completely destroy New York City. Faced with its unstoppable power, my Web of Tomorrow will rule this country within a month."

"Anton. Now it is your turn to listen to me. Of all the Group, I have found only your genius on a par with mine. You could become great in that new world. Join with me. Help me complete the Intensifier of your own free will. If not…" He looked with emphasis upon the zombie helmets.

Anton Macek closed his eyes and swallowed. He knew that everything depended upon the next thing he said.

"No, Emil," he breathed out firmly. "I shall not."

Janus leaned back and seemed to sigh. "So be it. Put the caps upon them!"

Clutched in the hands of the Maton-Men, Hardy and Macek struggled valiantly as the zombies who had searched them came forward again, each holding the gun-metal skullcap. But to no avail. Slowly, inexorably, the metal covers were forcibly jammed deep over their hair. For a moment, both shivered as if an electrical shock was passing through their bodies. Then their eyes grew blank. They stood aright, straight and stiff as ramrods, eyes locked straight ahead. Not a quiver of emotion showed on either face.

"Very well, Macek," The Recluse directed. "You shall begin plugging the last of the algorithms into the calculating machine. Horworth shall oversee the last of the calibrations. And, you—" He pointed to one of the white-coated Maton-Men who served as technician. "Take Hardy to Storeroom Four. I'll deal with him when I have the time."

The slave pulled the entranced Hardy away. Unresistingly the former criminologist followed his fellow zombie off the bridge.

As Macek silently began punching in figures into the calculator, The Brown Recluse stared at the robot-like form of his former friend almost sadly. Then, with a dismissive shrug, he turned to Horworth.

"Get them busy on the Intensifier. I want it operational within the hour. It is time the world heard from the Web of Tomorrow!"

Dizzy didn't know what had happened to her boss, but she knew it couldn't be good.

She hadn't heard from him in hours, and she just knew he was in trouble. Damn the man, anyway. Didn't he know what he did to her when he gallivanted off on another one of his hair-brained schemes?

She crushed out the sixth cigarette she had lit in as many minutes and sighed. Well, there wasn't anything to do but wait. Leaning back wearily in her chair, she realized her stomach was growling. She hadn't had supper yet.

Her favorite kosher deli was only a block away and a nice knish would really hit the spot. Grabbing her purse she abandoned the office, praying Kent wouldn't call for help in the meantime.

Saturday nights are always busy in Manhattan. The sidewalks were crowded with pedestrians, some making their way to restaurants or theatres, some to movie shows, many just out for the sheer joy of escaping their steel-and-concrete prisons. Everywhere she looked the storefronts

*Hardy and Macek stood aright, straight and stiff as ramrods, eyes locked straight ahead. Not a quiver of emotion showed on either face.*

and businesses were lit with the pulsating glow of neon, shining the streets like earthbound stars. The sights and sounds of the city at night, the rush of a million different lives all jumbled and mixed, always made Dizzy's blood pump a little faster. Yes, she was a New Yorker through and through. And proud of it.

A small form was slipping along the sidewalk weaving in and out between walkers. A stray dog some of the locals left food out for occasionally. It was thin and scrawny. As it came near, it suddenly stopped, shook its head, and whimpered as if something was bothering it. Dizzy reached out a hand to pat him. As she did, it shook his head again, more violently this time, and then threw back his head and started to howl, a howl of misery and pain. And the howling didn't stop.

Simultaneously, Dizzy became aware of a shrill ringing in her ears. Exactly like that when she had been exposed to the prototype Intensifier, but much, much sharper. A hundred times sharper.

The girl put her hands to her ears, grimacing. But the ringing only grew. Pain like heated knives shot through her brain. Unable to help herself, she stumbled as the ringing became more and more shrill, down to her knees, covering her head. Everyone else on the sidewalk were doing the same. The dog howled and howled, and the ringing kept right on growing. God, what was going on?

Gnashing her teeth against the ringing, Dizzy rolled over on her back, squinting her watering eyes. Then she saw something so horrifying she almost forgot the pain. With a scream, she pointed upward.

Far above, the tops of the skyscrapers surrounding the street were *quaking.*

The Marconi Field Intensifier was screeching with its own power.

No longer upon his throne, but standing next to the windows gazing down at toward the lighted spires of New York, The Brown Recluse exulted in his power! The nozzle of the Intensifier pointing through the open hatch downward, he could practically see the massively powerful radio waves emitting from the barrel of the gun-like monstrosity; each light and coil and gauge thrummed with energy!

He threw out his hands like a priest offering benediction. "Today it begins!"

Kent Hardy stood stiff and at attention amid the boxes and crates of a darkened storeroom. He made no movement, no sound. He simply stared ahead with his living dead face, the zombie cap weighing down upon his scalp.

For the longest time, nothing happened.

Except for something very peculiar.

First, Hardy's eyes flicked to the right. Then the left. As soon as he ascertained he truly was alone, his lips moved into a wide grin. Then he reached up and lightly plucked the skullcap from his hair!

When the Professor had caught him pomading his hair earlier, Hardy had actually been doing more than that. He had added something very special to the mix. While Macek was busy elsewhere, Hardy had briefly gone into town and purchased a box of extremely tiny magnetic bearings.

He had mixed these liberally with his can of Fancy's Sam's, then applied the mess to his hair. There had been methods behind his madness. Hardy knew that magnetism could often interfere with radio transmissions. Since the zombie skullcaps were powered by radio waves, he had theorized that possibly magnetism might disrupt them. Fortunately, he had been proven right.

Hardy had known The Brown Recluse would realize his "trap" was false. He had figured on being captured, taken to the villain's headquarters, and probably even enslaved. It had all been part of his plan. If The Recluse had captured him and then believed him helpless, he would have a free hand to stop him! He wished he could have been able to tell Macek, but its success depended on an acting ability he knew the Professor lacked.

It had been a risky maneuver, and Hardy knew it. But it had worked. Now he had to find some way to rescue Macek and Roe, and destroy the Intensifier. He had waited too long to ensure he hadn't been found out as it was, and The Recluse was probably already utilizing the device to endanger millions.

Carefully he checked the storeroom door. It was not locked; why should it have been? A Maton-Man was harmless without orders. Cracking it open, Hardy dared a quick peek. It was empty. Time to move. Slipping the dysfunctional cap back on, he once more made his face an emotionless blank. Then he stepped out from the storeroom and commenced walking, forcing the steady pace of the zombified slave, toward the bridge. He was counting that no one would pay any attention to a mindless Maton-Man walking down the aisle!

He wished he had his revolver, but there was no helping that now. All he could depend on was his wits and his fists. But he had to stop the

Recluse. Too many innocent lives were depending on him.

Only once did another zombie pass him, mindlessly lost in his own task. Hardy thanked his lucky stars.

There. The entrance to the bridge. Now the risk really began. The door would open automatically at his approach. His only hope was that The Recluse could never be bothered to look at the faces of his own slaves. Could he simply walk in as a zombie?

There was only one way to find out.

The panels slid open with a soft *whoosh.* Hardy paused for the slightest of milliseconds. Then: *In for a penny, in for a pound.* Keeping his face as immobile as possible, he marched with steady steps right into the lion's den.

A chill of horror ran down his spine.

The Intensifier had been activated! His ears throbbed like drums about to burst as its strength grew, beaming more and more invisible death down toward the helpless city below. And, walking around with calmly, as if they were simply doing some minor calibrations to an unimportant lab device, Professor Macek moved blank-faced around the Intensifier, zombie caps firm upon his head.

It was fortunate his steps did not take him near the open hatchway the barrel of the Intensifier poked downward to. One slip and he would fall thousands of feet and never even realize it.

But the two he most needed to know about, The Recluse and Horworth, stood facing the great window of the bow, gazing with rapturous joy at their work. Even with his mask on, Hardy could guess the gloating countenance upon Janus's face!

None had noticed him. The other Maton-Men on the bridge were too mesmerized by their own tasks. Fighting to keep his own face blank, sweat ran down Hardy's face as he strained to come up with some idea of what to do next. Then the words came back to him again.

*It must be that inducer coil again. Every time that goes, the whole thing shorts out."*

Horworth's own words! The inducer coil! Its failure had almost set the prototype on fire. And now he could see this infernal machine's own version, glowing red-hot with the energy racing along its copper skin. Hardy knew that if he did what he was about to do, he would probably never get off this ship alive. But for the millions of people far, far below, he knew he had no choice.

Once more he removed his zombie cap. Weighing it carefully in his hand, he judged the angle and distance to the coil. Then, throwing with all the strength he had used to toss forward passes back at Yale, he lobbed the thing right at the Intensifier!

His aim was true. The cap struck the inducer coil like a bowling ball hitting a pin, knocking straight off the Intensifier. As it snapped, sparks flew from the machine and a high-pitched whine moaned through the bridge.

Simultaneously, Hardy darted forward, yanking Macek from his place. He swept the skullcap from his head. Macek shook like an electric jolt had just flowed through him, but awareness and emotion returned to his face. "Kent, dear boy!"

"Never mind me!" hollered Hardy. "Do whatever you can to shut down this machine!"

"*HARDY! NO!!!*"

With a scream Janus had turned and witnessed everything that had happened. "Maton-Men! Seize him!" Ever obedient to their master, every remaining slave on the bridge turned and began racing to bring the criminologist down. But Hardy was already moving, plowing into the faceless mass like a rocket. As one slammed to the floor, he struck another; as he struck one, it fell to the floor like a downed tree. The problem was there were just too many Maton-Men crowding together in too small a space. Instead of overwhelming Hardy, they just got into each other's way. Hardy threw off as many zombie caps as he could, but many of the Maton-Men had had theirs on too long. The jolts they felt as the helmets were removed knocked them unconscious rather than regaining their humanity.

"*STOP HIM!!!*"screamed Janus in cold fury.

Macek was doing his share. Sweeping up spanners, screwdrivers, wrenches, anything he could find, he went at the Intensifier like a man insane. Gears and switches buckled beneath his fury. The acrid scent of smoke filled the chaotic bridge. Sparks flew. The Intensifier let off a grinding howl as its other coils grew white-hot.

"Janus! It's going to explode!" Horworth shouted. "We've got to get out of here!"

The Recluse ignored him. "Hardy! Get Hardy!"

Horworth slapped a hand upon Janus' shoulder. "We've got to get *out!*"

At the touch The Brown Recluse shuddered as if he were wearing one of his own helmets. With a roar he turned to face his flunky. "*YOU TOUCHED ME!*"

"Janus, you fool! Can't you see we're—"

"*NEVER—TOUCH—ME!!*" Janus' hands went to his holsters. Two sharp cracks shrilled out. Horworth staggered back, hand to his chest, blood spurting between his fingers. Like a man blind he stumbled, closer and closer to the Intensifier.

"Horworth! The hatch!" Macek cried.

Too late. In his dying stumbles the traitorous scientist had not seen how close he was. He yowled as he tumbled forth into the night.

But Macek had no time to waste upon him. For with a sudden shower of white sparks, the entire Intensifier burst into flames. The Professor yelped and drew back quickly: "I think I did a too good a job!" Red-orange flame flowed from the machine, across the floor and along the roof, casting everything it touched into blazes as it went.

"JANUS! IT'S OVER!" Hardy screamed as he finished off the last zombie. "WE'VE GOT TO GET OFF THIS DIRIGIBLE! YOU MUST HAVE PARACHUTES! WHERE ARE THEY??"

With eerie calm The Brown Recluse suddenly went silent. With deliberate movements and Hardy's astonished eyes he went and sat very carefully down upon his throne. Then in a malicious hiss that reverberated across the entire bridge he said:

"Find them yourself, Hardy."

Then he pressed a certain button on his armchair.

The throne fell into space as yet another hatch yawned open from beneath it. The Recluse fell with it, deathly silent, the only sign of emotion the hate in his glittering gray eyes as he vanished.

*My god,* Hardy thought incredulously.

But he could spare no further time on that. "Professor! There must be parachutes somewhere! We've got to find them!" Swiftly he crossed the bridge to a set of cabinets, feverishly throwing open drawers and doors.

"I found them!" Macek yelled, hauling out folded parcels of silk. "But there's only two!"

*For Janus and Horworth,* Hardy realized grimly. Janus had not intended on saving his slaves in case of accident.

Macek realized it as the same time. "There's Maton-Men all over this ship. There's no way we can save all them!"

A look a purest anger on his face, Hardy swung his parachute on. He knew he would never forgive himself for this. Nor would he ever forgive Janus. But there was no other choice.

"Go!" he cried, and raced for the open hatch the throne had fallen through. With a cry he hurled himself through it and into space, feeling the cold air whip across his body as he fell. After him came Macek.

Even as they dropped through, the Marconi Field Intensifier gathered itself for a last inferno. As the final bits of metal blew, the flames finally penetrated through the cabin roof to the silk balloon of the dirigible proper—and the flammable hydrogen gas inside. With a shattering explosion that lit up the night *The Spider's Eye* erupted, creating a final end to the schemes of an insane criminal.

"We did it, my boy!" the Professor yelled triumphantly through the whistling air. "We did it!"

But Kent Hardy made no reply.

Smoothly the black limousine came to a halt before the unobtrusive brownstone almost beneath the shadow of the Empire State Building. Two men in dark suits climbed out of the front seats. The first opened the back, pulled out and set up a wheelchair, then assisted the man in the back seat into it.

New Yorkers are nothing if not resilient. Barely a week had passed since a new star had blazed over the Manhattan sky that things had returned to business as usual. If you had asked Hardy about it, he would have just shrugged. This was New York City—in its day it had seen masked marauders, murderous purple lights, skyscraper phantoms, and even a giant monkey. What was some nutcase with a radio death ray? Within a month the whole matter would have been forgotten.

But the man in the wheelchair, who was not a native New Yorker, was taking the matter very seriously. And he was determined such like it would never happen again.

"Kent Hardy's office."

The man in the wheelchair spoke, with a rich, cultured, plummy voice. "I should like to know if Mr. Hardy is available. And Professor Macek, if that is possible. I understand he's staying here."

"Do you have an appointment?"

"I'm afraid not. Nevertheless, I believe they will see me. Tell you what, young lady. Why don't you come to the door and take a gander, and then you can decide."

A pause. Then: "What the heck; it's your nickel." After a moment Dizzy opened the door and took her gander at the man in the wheelchair.

"YIPES!" she declared without preamble.

The man in the wheelchair smiled. "Mr. Hardy?" he encouraged.

"Uh—uh—I mean, yes, *Sir!* Come right in! I'll—I'll get Mr. Hardy!"

The man in the wheelchair's grin grew wider and he allowed his guardians to push him into the hall. Moments later a flushed Kent Hardy and Professor Anton Macek, followed by a still flustered Dizzy, came running up to greet him.

"Mr—Mr..." Hardy could not spit the word out. "This is...I'm honored!"

"Oh, my...oh, dear!" was the only thing Macek could add.

"Mr. Hardy....Professor Macek," their guest nodded. "I'm the one who should be honored. Oh–and do forgive the unexpected surprise of my disability. I don't make it a habit to let people know I'm wheelchair-bound. Appearances, you know."

In spite of his surprise, Hardy remembered his manners. "There's nothing to forgive, Sir. May we get you something? Coffee, tea?"

"No—no thank you. I'm afraid I can only stay a few minutes, and I really don't want anyone to know I came here. But I wished to thank you both personally for your actions against this 'Brown Recluse' character. You have done this country a great service."

"Oh, Sir," the Professor said. "It was really nothing."

"I disagree, Professor. Saving this city from utter destruction and the very country from a madman's blackmail is hardly 'nothing.'"

"But that is what I came to speak with you about. After a thorough investigation, my advisers have informed me they regard any further threat from Dr. Janus as over. He is undoubtedly dead. Very few people could survive flinging themselves out of a dirigible, after all." He smiled sardonically.

Hardy folded his arms. "I have to agree that it's highly unlikely he's still alive, Sir."

The personage regarded the criminologist through half-lidded eyes. "But not *impossible*, young man?"

For a moment, Hardy looked toward his old mentor for inspiration. Macek simply shook his head. Hardy sighed, nodded, and turned back to his guest. "No, Sir. *Not* impossible."

"The Brown Recluse is insane, but he is not stupid. He would never just let himself drop out of even a burning dirigible without some sort of backup. What that was I cannot begin to guess, but I'm certain he must have had one. And as you said yourself, the body has yet to be recovered. Professor Macek and I have been discussing it, and we have both come to the same conclusion—Dr. Janus will be back. Count on it."

Their guest sighed deeply, removed his glasses, and gently wiped them. "Very well," he said at last, "I concur. It seems super-criminals like him are coming out of the woodwork these days. The Black Star, Dr. Satan, the Whispering Shadow, the Tiger Shark…the list seems to go on and on. All we need is a new one.

"But this contraption of his, this Marconi Field Intensifier—that's destroyed once and for all, yes?"

"That I can verify, Sir," replied the Professor. "With the rest of my colleagues…gone, there is no one left with the complete set of algorithms needed to operate the machine. And I have destroyed the prototype."

The man in the wheelchair nodded. "Well, at least that's something to be thankful for. Then I can take my leave with a lighter heart. Thank you— all of you.

"But I would leave you with one request. You say there's still a chance The Recluse might surface again. If ever that day does come—can I count on you, the three of you, to be there to stop him?"

He regarded his hosts with an expectant smile.

Once more Kent Hardy looked to his old teacher, then to his secretary.. The Professor coughed and, despite himself, grinned. Dizzy popped her gum and rolled her eyes to heaven. Then the young criminologist reached out, took his visitor's hand, and shook it was an eternal promise.

"Mr. President—I don't think there would be any way we *couldn't*."

# THE END

*BUT THE BROWN RECLUSE SHALL STRIKE AGAIN…*

# I LOVE PULP BADDIES

I owe Ron Fortier big time for his patience for this.

Three years ago at PulpFest I offered him a character concept for a villain that could run through all the titles of Airship 27 Productions; a master criminal that could alternately encounter Dan Fowler, Secret Agent X, the Moon Man, and the rest of our entourage, to be used by an author so long as the character wasn't killed off. A villain calling himself The Brown Recluse.

Instead, Ron offered me a compromise. With the creation of *Mystery Men (and Women)*, he pointed out there was an opening for a story about The Recluse there. After all, mystery men don't always have to be *heroes*. Villains as protagonists have been a long staple of pulp culture, from Fantomas to Raffles to Fu Manchu to Dr. Satan. So long as there's an effective hero to fight them, why not?

Why not, indeed?

So I agreed to write the first adventure of The Brown Recluse. I knew quite a bit of what I wanted. I knew it was going to be a salute to the great movie serials of the 1930s and 1940s with their mystery villains and outlandish contraptions, and I knew pretty much what The Recluse's costume would be.

And, really, that was it.

And for three years, I started, and trashed, and started, and trashed, and started, and trashed. The story just wasn't *working*, and I didn't know why.

The hero went through a mass of permutations. For the longest time, he was going to be Victor Yu, a heroic Chinese-American. I've always wanted to do a "reverse yellow peril" story, where an Eastern hero fights a white villain, and thought this might be a good way to do it. But somehow, no matter how I tried, Victor didn't seem to fit here. He yet lives—I plan on using him in another potential series I feel he works better in—but I realized that I needed a *movie serial* hero to make this work. Someone like—well, Ralph Byrd, who played Dick Tracy in several series and B-movies of the period. And then it hit me—why not actually make it Ralph Byrd? Enter Kent Hardy, and suddenly things started snapping.

Secondly, I finally realized I was reaching too much with my villain. Originally The Brown Recluse was to be head of a secret society of technocratic terrorists called The Web of Tomorrow. But introducing that concept, with all the back story it promised, proved problematic in the short amount of space I had to work with. Besides, most movie serial villains worked alone, with just a few thugs to command. Reluctantly, I decided to shift the Web itself out, although there's no saying The Recluse might not found it in a future tale!

Regardless, Ron patiently waited for me to finally get this thing going. Ron, I can't tell you how grateful I am for that. Thank you for your kindness and friendship, and thank you for giving a very slow author a chance to finally get this thing right

For the record, in addition to Ralph Byrd as Kent Hardy, the physical appearance of The Brown Recluse is based off serial and movie villain Lionel Atwill, Dizzy—very loosely—off comedienne Joan Davis, and Professor Macek off the Peter Cushing version of Dr. Who from the *Dalek* movies. The careful reader might also note some tips-of-the-hat to other pulp series and movie serials. Hope you like it. Hope it was worth the wait. The Brown Recluse *will* return–but this time, at a much faster pace!

GREG GICK - is a pulp writer from Lafayette, Indiana. His work has appeared in the SECRET AGENT X and MARS MCCOY anthologies from Airship 27, and TALES OF THE SHADOWMEN from Black Coat Press. He gets his ideas from donning a mask and cloak at night and hunting criminals while laughing maniacally. Chicks dig that sort of thing. Really.

# KIRI

## "Night of the Mist"
### By Curtis Fernlund

Manhattan
December, 1936

As always and no matter the hour or the weather the Hudson docks were a buzz of activity. Leaden gray clouds hung low in the sky, thick and roiling, reflecting the glare of city lights and work lamps lining the river and blotting out the stars and moon, frigid air threatening snow by morning. Great chunks of ice floated down the Hudson towards the mouth and New York Harbor making travel on the river hazardous but doing little to stem the steady flow of trade ships looking for berth at the bustling wharves, dozens plying the waters along the Manhattan and New Jersey sides alike.

Despite the cold men were out in force, the docks never shutting down merely slowing with the rise and fall of the tide. Trucks rattled along the old, cobbled roads transporting goods to the warehouses that lined the avenues and side streets that paralleled the river, wares and goods imported from the world over, everything from foodstuffs to textiles, clothing to exotic fascinations. Burly, haggard workers dressed in layers against the cold plied ropes and pulleys, shouting orders and cautions in a myriad of accents as net-meshed bundles swung high and over the old, worn wood, other bundles and boxes carted away on dolly and jack to disappear into the deep shadows of the store houses beyond.

Another normal night along the West Side Hudson docks...

Kiri sighed and leaned back against the cold stone at her back. She felt the chill of the brick even through her thick, woolen longcoat as she took a sip of water from the silver snifter that she had brought along in her pocket. She was cold, her limbs aching in the chill winter air, her breath clouding as she lazily watched the activity on the wharves just over a block away from her perch on the cornice of one of the many Cunard Line warehouses that lined the Hudson Docks. Another fruitless watch, a normal, wasted night with little sleep ahead and even less to show for her efforts.

But of course she had to follow every lead, every clue or rumor that passed her way no matter how trivial or preposterous. She could never take the chance that any lead might pan out. It was a matter of debt to repay and honor to restore.

She had received a tip from one of her stoolies "Old Rog" hustling

Times Square and the Theater District on a blustery Christmas Day just a few days past that a load of "Chinee" *pen yen* was rolling into Slip Fifty-Seven come midnight or so on *The Shiro* out of Japan and that the "scumster" that she was looking for, had been looking for, for years, was involved somehow and might surface. He might show up, and even that was a chance she would have to take, a lead she needed to follow no matter how slim the odds. She had dropped the legless veteran of the Great War a Lincoln and thanked him, though she had doubted that the tip would pan out in the end. She had watched Rog wheel away on his raggedy, low-wheeled platform rattling his battered tin cup at the tourists, then started making plans for the long night ahead that she would spend watching the berth in question.

Two hours past midnight and chilled to the bone Kiri stretched and yawned ready to call it a night. *The Shiro* had arrived at half past the hour of twelve and the ship's crew and dockworkers had set to task unloading the cargo with the usual Japanese efficiency. If the opium had been unloaded and distributed she had not seen it, nor did she care. If the denizens of New York City wanted to squander their money in these hard times of Depression and rattle their senses with delusional drugs, that was their business. Kiri did not care for the opium, but rather the man rumored to be involved. The man that she had been hunting across two continents for over twenty years. The devil that had ravaged her *dojo* and home and changed her life forever.

Chiba Prefecture
Japan
Years Earlier

She was sobbing and could not catch her breath.

Suwan Shin*obi* shivered as she held the wad of her shredded *kimono* to the gash running the length of her left fore arm. Blood seeped into the silken robe as she gripped her *obi* in gritted teeth, pulling the sash tight to hold the packing in place, knotting it off with numb, fumbling fingers. The bitter scent of iron filled the air mingling with *Sensei*'s favored mint herbs and flowered incense making her head swim and her sight waver with the loss of blood. She was sweating and weak, fading towards unconsciousness as she heard mocking laughter and looked up.

The beast stood before her, Sensei's prized pupil holding her father's *katana* in hand. The silver blade gleamed in the dull, cloudy light of the *dojo*, the runes etched into the metal sparkling blood red as he held it mockingly before her, examining its strength and beauty.

"A marvelous blade," he hissed sneering as he turned the flat to the light making it sparkle and flare as though afire. "Far too good to be in the hands of your doddering father. A blade of this renown, forged by the master Masamune deserves a true owner and host. A true master."

Suwan looked about at the carnage in the small, simple dwelling trying to stay awake. Her peers were slaughtered, her friends and fellows bled and ravaged, their cooling bodies strewn about by the demon secreted in their midst. Her own father, her Sensei and teacher lay dead on the blood-soaked mats covering the oaken floor, his headless body steaming in the chill of fall air. She choked back a sob, her hand scrambling for the discarded sword at her side. She would have vengeance. The *Gaki* laughed at her efforts as her fingers wrapped about the tightly woven leather cords of the grip as she tried to raise her own *katana*.

His foot slammed down on the blade easily pinning it to the floor. Suwan struggled to raise the metal, to turn the edge but she did not have the strength. She looked up hopelessly through bleary eyes into the grinning visage of the demon.

"You would be wise to desist, little one," he said as he slipped the stolen blade through the sash of his own *obi*. He waved his hand about the slaughterhouse. "Your friends and fellows failed to stop me. I have slain them all, including your master, your father. What chance have you, child, a slip of a girl not even fully trained in the ways of *Bushido* and the arts of the *samurai*?"

Suwan stared at her friends. At her dead friends and hung her head. Sobbing again as the *Gaki* knelt at her side. Smirking wickedly he grabbed a handful of her jet-black hair and jerked her head roughly back.

"And now, lest you forget, something to remember me by." Suwan gasped staring through tear-filled eyes as Hana leaned closer, his sallow skin darkening, face elongating to accommodate his suddenly long and jagged teeth.

Pain as he bit into her still bleeding arm, burning as her warm blood gushed forth. Feeling his tongue as it probed the wound, suckling. Suwan screamed.

Kiri blinked, starting awake and knuckling the sleep from her eyes as she peered down at the docks, trying to focus. She had fallen asleep and something had wrenched her from her nightmares though at a glance she could not tell what. Light still glared from the wharves and men still bustled about. A foghorn sounded from the harbor as a light snow had begun to fall. Everything seemed as it had before. But then she saw.

A long, sleek, black car had pulled to idle at the edge of the cobbled side street; plumes of exhaust billowing from its tailpipe in the freezing air. Five men had stepped from the huge Lincoln, all dressed in long coats and hats, wide brims pulled low as they surveyed the activity about *The Shiro*. Four were white men, but one was Oriental she could easily see; a Boss and his bodyguards by the look; three Rubbers, professional killers no doubt, gangsters all. The thugs held guns she could see, one a sawed-off shotgun, another a greasegun partially hidden in the flapping tails of his long coat, the submachine gun ready to be brought to bear, the third a pistol. They made no attempt to hide their weapons as they stepped along the docks, fanning out to protect their employer, heads shifting as they scanned the area. The Boss amongst them was a fat man, his own, buttoned longcoat bulging tightly over his rotund girth as he chewed on a cigar watching the activity, a black bowler hat pulled to his brow. It was the third man however that drew Kiri's attention finally, all of her focus.

She could feel her heart hammering in her chest as her slender hand slipped into the deep pockets of her coat pulling free the small set of binoculars that Diane had given her just last Christmas. "Figure they'll come in handy some day," Diane had said with a wide smile to see Suwan's delight. She had been right of course, as always.

Kiri peered through the twin scopes, turning the dial with her finger to bring the scene into clarity, ignoring the three hoods and lighting on the Boss just a moment. William 'Hoss' Horton as she had expected by his profile and telltale hat, a greasy politician and the loudest voice in Mayor La Guardia's City Council; he had his fingers in every illegal operation in the city, rumor said. Though of course nothing had ever been proven. Diane had said often and vehemently that he was a rat through and through, running guns and liquor, and apparently opium into the city, dealing in prostitution of both women and children, men and boys. She would tell Diane later what she had seen, but 'Boss Hoss' was not her concern tonight. She scanned left to the last man, ignoring the gunsels again, to the Oriental and her heart skipped a beat as she focused on his face, another shiver rippling down her spine.

Kareta Hana was handsome still. His chiseled face cold in the harsh glare of the work lights, impassive as he scanned the docks watching the opium being unloaded from the *Shiro*. Dark hair poked from the edges of his wide-brimmed hat, a thin cigarette dangling from his pale lips framed by a thinly trimmed mustache and beard. Kiri could see his hand on the pommel of his sword mostly hidden beneath his coat; the sword stolen from her murdered father. His dark eyes flicked and flickered in the garish light, scanning the wharves and surrounds, eventually resting on her as he stared at the old warehouses lining the docks. She saw him grin. She felt the burn of the mark on her arm hidden beneath her boiled leather bracer, the wound that had never healed.

Kiri was scrambling down the side of the building, rappelling on the thin line she had affixed down the face of the warehouse, the rope wrapped under her right thigh, across her body and over her left shoulder. Her leather riding boots hit the damp stone with a heavy thump and she was running, her hand sliding her own *katana* from its scabbard at her leather belt, her blade flashing in the stark, artificial light as she pulled it free. Flakes of snow swirled in her wake as she ran, dark eyes wide with desire and anger, tasting blood.

Hoss Horton turned at the sound of clamping feet on the slick cobblestones. He stared in disbelief, eyes bulging comically at the sight before him, a slip of a Chinee girl running at him with a sword held high. He puffed on his cigar, rolling it to the corner of his thick lips. "What the hell is this?" he asked incredulously and Hana laughed. The lead hood pulled his Tommygun free of his concealing coat and leveled it at the girl racing towards them; his fellows following suit just a heartbeat behind. About the docks the workers nearest paused, some pulling freight hooks free of the crates they were hauling, steering poles and knives popping into view, ready to defend. Hana ignored the sudden tension and casually placed a hand on the barrel of the lead hood's gun, pointing the barrel down.

"This is mine," he hissed grinning almost lecherously. He drew his own sword in a fluid motion and raised it to point, then to guard as Kiri was swiftly upon him.

Her first blow slashed wildly, forgetting all of her training, Hana easily countering her vicious attack and thrusting her blade aside with little effort, just a slight flick of his wrist. She recovered quickly though, spinning and slicing towards his midsection, but again he easily, casually blocked her assault with a down-turned blade. Steel met steel clanging in the night, metal sparking on metal as Hana shoved her back and away. Kiri staggered and set en guard with her blade hovering horizontally overhead, breathing hard and staring daggers at the man that had destroyed her life. Hana laughed again, a cruel thing that cut to her soul.

"Little Mist," he mocked, grinning widely as he angled his own blade to counter hers, "you have learned nothing after all these years. I am your better. I always have been. I always will be. Accept your failure and disgrace and put it to the past."

"No!" Kiri shouted, sword flashing as she waded into the demon, the *Gaki*, her nemesis and bane. "Never surrender!!" Her sword flashed whipping wildly as she struck high then low, a flurry of motion as she kicked and punched, calling on all of her training. Hana grinned as his own sword flickered meeting her assault, easily turning aside every lunge and slash. Finally he leaned in and trapped Kiri's blade, thrusting it aside and away, giving it a casual glance as it spiraled off to clatter on the docks a few yards distant. With a flick of his wrist his own sword pressed into the soft of her throat drawing a pinprick of blood.

"I could kill you now," he whispered, "and I should, but you continue to amuse me. Keep struggling my little Mist. Make your father's cursed spirit proud."

Hana shifted his stance and the pommel of his sword slammed into her temple. Kiri fell to the damp cold wood of the docks, blessed oblivion washing over her.

"Gaggh!"

Kiri screamed startling awake at the shock of the icy cold water. Colder than anything she had ever known or experienced, beyond reckoning. Eyes wide with sudden panicked fright she kicked and clawed struggling as the frigid darkness swallowed her, washing over her, threatening to consume her whole and dragging her down. Water flowed into her gaping mouth clogging her lungs, choking her as she tried to gasp for a breath that would not come. Panicked she thrashed and struggled.

With a soundless thump that rattled her bones her feet found purchase and she kicked, jumped, her freezing, numbing body thrusting upwards amidst billowing clouds of silt off the river bottom. She broke the surface of the river gagging, bile spewing as she hacked and coughed, gasping for air. Tears welled in her eyes as she felt the current clutching at her again, trying to pull her back under, her clothes weighing her down. She writhed, trying to keep her head above the water, struggling to strip off her heavy, sodden longcoat.

Through her blurry vision she saw Hana standing at the edge of the rotting wooden dock watching her with amusement, blue cigarette smoke billowing about his face. She heard a voice over her own ragged breathing, her splashing as she tried to stay afloat desperately trying to shed her layers of clothing. Her muscles were growing fatigued already, numb in the icy waters of the Hudson, frozen. The lead hood stepped into view, a shadowy silhouette back lit by the distant work lamps, his image wavering in the swirl of windswept snow.

"Hoss is ready, Hana," the shadowy form said with a low gravelly voice. Kiri saw the man's gun wavering towards her as she dipped beneath the water again, then popping up, her leaden coat falling free at last. "Ya don't wanna off the dame outright, then let her die in peace."

"I will be along, Gideon," the *Gaki* said his gaze never straying from Kiri's struggles as he flicked his spent cigarette butt into the water before her. The other man shrugged and then hurried away, Hana smirking all the while. He squatted at the dock's edge almost teetering on the brink with his arms folded and resting on his knees as he looked down. "You try so hard, a true samurai at heart if not in name. Death before dishonor, vengeance and dedication to your Lord, obligation. A lost way, an art, and one you would do well to abandon... if you wish to survive, of course."

The demon stood laughing, pulling another thin cigarette from the inner folds of his coat. He put it to his lips as Kiri sank beneath the waves again, splashing furiously and trying to stay afloat. She saw a flare of red that slowly faded away.

Numb fingers wrapped about the old slick wood, curling and gripping for purchase as Kiri heaved, pulling herself from the icy grasp of the Hudson. She gasped sweet, fresh air, vomiting bile as she strained, pulling her numb and listless body from the frigid river, inch by inch, rung by rung.

Finally she heaved forward and collapsed on the rotting wood of the docks, breathing hard and sobbing. She had almost died; almost, caught in the river's grip, sucked into its black, icy depths. It had been pure luck that she had snagged the edge of the pier and dragged her body, frozen and numb to the ladder, up and out. She had almost died, but worse, she had failed. Again.

Kiri lay on the edge of the docks panting for breath, shivering in the cold and cursing herself. She had had him. Hana had been before her and she could have killed him but she had let emotions rule and he had bested her again, and made her look the fool, the child. Never again.

Taking long deep breaths she got her energy back, her mind focused. She saw her *katana* lying to the side, discarded and broken in two by the *Gaki* on the wharves, a final slap in the face. He considered her nothing; less than nothing, a distraction at best; an amusement. Kiri reached for the shattered sword and gripped it wrapping her fingers about the hilt, feeling the cool leather, squeezing her fist as the blood in her veins started to circulate and burn again.

"I'll find you," she hissed, her voice ragged and hoarse, teeth chattering. She spat. "I'll find you again, and kill you, demon. On my father's soul, on his grave, you are dead." She repeated the vow that she had sworn years ago, the promise that drove her and ruled her life.

Even so it was a long time before Kiri found the strength to rise and finally stagger off into the night. And all about her the docks buzzed with activity.

"Well, you look like death warmed over."

Suwan Shin*obi* forced a weak smile to her lips as she shuffled into the dining room. She was still freezing despite the warmth of the Pulitzer brownstone bordering Washington Square Park and overlooking the last remaining Arch dedicated to Commodore George Dewey and his victories in the Pacific during the Spanish-American War. She was still in her long, flannel night dress, an equally long cotton robe over that tied at the waist and a pair of fur-lined terrycloth slippers on her feet as she made her way into the room to stand with her back to the hissing radiator, luxuriating in the warmth it gave off. She knew that her long, black hair must be a frazzled mess pulled back into a bun and held loosely in place with the dry quill of a fountain pen, her face bland and pale, dark, puffy bags under her almond eyes and a goose egg blushing at the edge of her temple. She did not care.

It had taken over an hour for her to make her way downtown again from Hell's Kitchen to Greenwich Village, freezing every step of the way after her near drowning in the Hudson River. She had been dripping wet as she had hurried east from the docks as best as she could manage, flagging taxicabs that had sped past ignoring her. Not that she could blame them, given her ragged, waterlogged state of appearance.

She had eventually stumbled into the Saint Ignatius Church Soup Kitchen on 9th Avenue at 39th for a bit of needed warmth and rest, surprised to find its doors unlocked and open giving aid at such a late hour. She had seen upon entering that the pews were full almost shoulder to shoulder, the homeless and destitute finding sanctuary as an older, gray-haired man passed amongst them offering comfort and salvation to those yet awake and wanting. Shivering she had huddled under a coarse blanket while the priest, Father William, offered her hot tea and a dry bed for the night.

"We are always here to help," he had said smiling as he set a steaming bowl of lentil soup before her, more water than bean, and a heel of stale bread. "I wish we had more to offer, but times are hard, as you well know, I'm sure. Still, God provides." Kiri nodded, thanking the old priest with a smile as she ate, relishing the warm food and the thick, scratchy blanket.

"Do you need a place to stay for the night? We have beds, though they're little more than cots, really." He shrugged, smiling. The Jesuit watched her as she finished the slight meal, finally standing on shaking legs. "You're still soaking wet. You'll die of pneumonia if you go back to the streets. Please stay." Kiri was touched by his concern.

"I have a home, downtown. I will not be on the streets long. I just have to get there and I will be fine." Kiri huddled in the blanket, the priest watching her from the far side of the table. Finally he nodded and began to clear away the dishes.

"Keep the blanket. I wish I had a spare coat to give you, but as I said, times are hard."

"I will be fine. Thank you for your kindness." Kiri bowed at the waist and had headed towards the door.

"Wait!" Father William had called out and Kiri paused, a slim hand on the ornate brass doorknob. The old, gray-haired priest jogged up, his hand digging in his pocket. He pressed a few pennies into the palm of her hand. "It's not much, but enough for the El. I doubt any hack in his right mind would stop for you this time of the morning, dressed as you are and soaked to the bone."

Kiri smiled, nodded. Moved again by the priest's concern and generosity. "Thank you," she had said. "I will pay you back." Father William waved her offer away.

"We're here to serve all of God's children. Stay safe, child."

Kiri had nodded and left, gasping at the chill as she huddled in her blanket and made her way further east to Times Square and the Elevated Train that ran the length of 6th Avenue. She caught the Independent Line riding the 'D' to the West 4th station then hoofing her way to the Pulitzer Manse just a few short blocks away from the stop. She had slipped in through the service entrance even as the first gray light of false dawn illuminated the horizon, lighting the thick winter clouds in shades of rose.

She had stripped out of her sodden clothes, wanting nothing more than a hot bath but settled for wrapping in her nightclothes after a quick washing and finally collapsing to her bed for a few, fitful hours of sleep before a new day dawned.

"Thank you, Diane," she replied with no little sarcasm lacing her voice.

She saw Diane Pulitzer smirk as she ruffled her newspaper, the morning edition of *The World News*, the daily paper that she owned. Suwan sidled towards the food trolley and poured herself a mug of steaming water over the green tea leaves that she preferred set out by Helga the housekeeper, bless her. As she stirred the leaves into the water, savoring the rising heat and the aroma, she rested back against the wall finally feeling a bit of warmth in her bones and tired muscles.

"Rough night, Dear?" Diane asked setting her paper aside and taking a bite of dark toast slathered with orange marmalade. Suwan nodded as she strained her tea through a cotton mesh then dropping the soiled strainer into the rubbish bin set beside the table. She took a sip of her tea and finally sat at the table in her usual place opposite her friend, confidante and employer.

She had known Diane Pulitzer for many years now, and the owner of *The World News* was one of the few people that knew of her other life, her secret life as a so-called 'Mystery Woman'; *Kiri the Mist*. They had met not long after Suwan had arrived in New York, on the trail of Hana almost fifteen years prior. She had followed the beast from San Francisco, where she had entered America by steam ship and trailed him eventually to Manhattan via the Atlantic/Pacific line cross country by rail, finally arriving in New York City's Grand Central Station one cold winter morning.

She remembered their first meeting, she wide-eyed at the grandeur that was Manhattan with its sky scrapers and dirty, bustling streets, Diane seasoned and gruff, already the owner and editor of the *News*, having inherited the paper and half of the fortunes of her journalist father, Joseph

Pulitzer who had passed in 1911. Diane had proven herself early on in the century following in the footsteps of the likes of Nelly Bly, becoming a hard-boiled investigative reporter in her own right, one of the first women to make a name for themselves in the field of journalism. Now almost forty-five years later she owned *The World News* and was semi-retired at the age of fifty-four, dabbling in editorials occasionally or actually reporting when necessity or the mood struck.

She was still a handsome woman, her curly red hair streaked and showing silver in places with laugh lines crinkling her skin about her full lips and dazzling blue eyes. She was a bit more robust than that day that they had first met in Grand Central Station when she had been following a lead on moonshine runners even as Suwan had stepped off the train. Diane had exposed the smugglers and they had opened fire with Tommyguns in the crowded terminal wounding dozens and killing without a care trying to escape. Suwan had drawn her blade and stopped the mayhem in a violent flurry of motion that had so impressed Diane that she had hired Suwan to be her confidante, for her as well as her daughter, Denise. Rather, her bodyguard, and Suwan had readily accepted.

Suwan had moved into the Pulitzer Manse, a brownstone on the fringes of Washington Square Park, which Diane had purchased after her father had passed, joining the staff, which consisted of Helga the housekeeper and cook, Lancaster the chauffeur and handy man and Rebecca the "tweenie" maid. Suwan's official title was tutor, and she was charged with teaching Diane's only daughter the ways of the world and whatever she could of the Japanese language and culture, which was fine though odd she thought. Her duties were actually few and left much time to hunt the demon that had become her obsession.

And the adventures they had shared over the years.

"I found Hana last night," Suwan said watching Diane's eyes widen in surprise. She set her coffee mug aside and leaned forward, excitement sparkling in her piercing gaze.

"Tell me," Diane hissed staring intently, listening as Suwan related the night's events. Her friend sighed, settling back as Suwan told of her failure, finally picking up the silver coffeepot from the trolley and refilling her mug.

"At least you know he's here, in town again." Diane added sugar and cream to her coffee, stirring the mixture. "And working with Horton, no less. Fat bastard! I wish I could find something to bring him down. Then your Hana would be out in the cold. He'll turn up again, I'm sure."

*"Tell me,"* Diane hissed staring intently.

"I know," Suwan said sipping at her tea. "I just need to find the connection." Suwan yawned. She was feeling better but still sleepy and tired, having only gotten two hours sleep at best.

"Follow the opium," Diane suggested. "It'll probably end up in the Chinatown Dens and the Lower East Side. Your Hana is probably Horton's main man down in the Oriental sector. He'll pop up."

"I've walked Chinatown many times," Suwan said. "The people do not accept me. They do not confide in me, because of my heritage I think, and my mark. They know I am an outsider. And it is a very close-knit community. If Hana is there, they hide him, protect him. He may even have some authority there, with the Tong and Yakuza. I have heard rumors of a warlord."

"Don't give up," Diane offered sipping at her coffee again. "Never surrender, right?"

Suwan smiled.

"Good morning."

Both Diane and Suwan looked up as Diane's daughter Denise strolled into the dining room. At eighteen she was a younger version of her mother cut from the same cloth. Curly red hair and a sparsely freckled face, stark blue eyes and a razor sharp mind, she stepped up to the table in her dressing gown and took a seat, pouring herself a coffee from the silver pot. Diane took the moment to light a cigarette from a silver case on the table, leaning back in her ladder-back chair and crossing her legs.

"Finally decided to get up, did we?"

"Mo-therrr..." Denise said drawing out the word as she buttered a slice of toasted bread, "It's Saturday. Surely you can allow me to sleep late just a bit?"

"In my day..." Diane began and Suwan smirked as the younger woman rolled her eyes, nibbling at her toast.

"In YOUR day you would be up at the crack of dawn, two hours before you went to bed the night before investigating some scandal. I know, I know. But it's not your day anymore. The days of Yellow Journalism are over. People want the facts, the *real* facts about what's happening in the city, and the country and the escalation in Europe. George the Sixth is King of England. Germany and Italy are Fascist States and Hitler's occupied the Rhineland again. The mobs are thick as thieves in Chicago, and it's not much better here with Horton running willy-nilly over the show in the shadows. Something needs to be done. Before the world goes to hell in a hand basket."

Suwan saw Diane's wide grin at her daughter's vehemence. The younger Pulitzer woman was a spitfire like her mother, never accepting anything at face value. Always digging for the story beneath the headlines.

"I cannot believe they are letting this Hitler run ramshod through Europe like he's doing. Have they forgotten the Great War so soon? There's rumors that he's culling the masses you know, herding the so-called inferior races into ghettoes. It's dreadful that the 'Powers That Be' can let that happen. Don't they care?" Denise seemed truly upset as she turned her mother's newspaper towards herself to scan the front-page stories.

"Not when money is involved," Diane offered, "and thus far this little bastard, Adolf Hitler, is good for business. He's turned Germany's economy towards the black again and employed the country's homeless and destitute in his rise. I've heard the likes of Bush and Rockefeller and others of the American elite have been investing in the 'New Germany'. Just what Hitler's goals are though is anyone's guess." Suwan sipped at her tea and looked at Diane, recognizing the face of grim determination that she knew so well. She could imagine that Diane would at least be writing editorials against the rumors seeping out of Europe and the rumblings of war in the wind.

"How's that paper coming?" Diane finally asked of her daughter, changing the subject. Denise Pulitzer was in her first year at New York University, studying creative writing, journalism and English wanting to follow in her mother's footsteps. Denise had a sharp mind and a flair with words and Suwan thought she would go far. Too she worked part time at *The World*, though only as a copy boy and gopher, and that only because her mother owned the paper. Despite the efforts of the likes of Nelly Bly and even Diane, the world of journalism was still mostly a male dominated career.

"I'm stumped," Denise said leaning back with a sigh. She nibbled at her piece of toast. "I think I may have bitten off more than I can chew. The benefits of feudalism over democracy are few and far between I think. I may need to reconsider my theme."

"Nonsense," Diane said taking a sip of coffee and a long drag from her cigarette. "It's a good idea. You just need to dig deeper." Diane smiled and looked at Suwan. "Or maybe speak to a more direct source."

Denise followed her mother's gaze and smiled widely at Suwan even as Helga bustled into the room and started clearing empty plates and silverware. The older woman was in her seventies but still active and robust, her chubby cheeks red and her brown eyes alert. "Will there be anything else, Madam?" she asked of Diane as she gathered the empty china.

"Only that you stop calling me Madam, Helga," Diane said with a smile. It was a recurring conversation between the publisher and the housekeeper, though something that Helga could never accept apparently. She huffed and brushed a stray strand of hair behind her ear.

"Of course, Ma'am." Suwan smirked as she felt a light touch on her arm. She turned to Denise.

"You'll help me?"

Suwan nodded. "Of course. Japan has only recently left feudalism behind in favor of Imperialism. I will be happy to share what I can."

"Hot dog!" Denise cheered, smiling and face beaming. Diane shook her head with a wide grin and went back to her paper.

"The samurai were made outlaw," Suwan continued as she whipped her *boken* about, slapping the wooden practice sword at the red-painted spots highlighted on the practice dummy in a quick flurry of motion. The target was tightly bound strands of straw shaped in the general form of a man, stick lashed to one hand and a wooden disk representing a shield lashed to the other arm. She was sweating despite the December chill and that she was dressed down into her silken under garb. Her long black hair was tied back into a bun that was coming loose. Her feet crunched in the light coating of snow underfoot there in the back courtyard of the Pulitzer Manse.

"The young, new emperor of the recently restructured empire unfortunately listened to advisors more interested in advancing their personal status and coffers than maintaining the old traditions that had served so well. Feudalism fell quickly to the pressures of the West and the errant dream of Capitalism." She slammed the wooden practice sword at the target's throat, ribs and thighs, spinning gracefully to bring the blade up in a defensive stance. Her breathing was calm and steady as she searched for a common thought, a "place" that would placate her burning emotions. In her heart she still fumed over the previous night's travesty.

"But surely the samurai fought back?" Denise said as she scribbled in her notebook. She was dressed in heels and a long pencil skirt, blouse and long overcoat against the winter chill. They were in the courtyard behind the Manse, Diane's garden that was all but dead caught tightly in winter's grip. Suwan slashed at the practice dummy and it writhed, spinning on its tether.

"They did," Suwan said as she slapped the wooden blade to the mannequin, tapping the red-coated highlights about the body; neck, chest and groin. She stepped back bringing her blade to bear hovering horizontally overhead. She flicked the practice sword to the side and stepped back with a slight bow to her non-living opponent. "But the new empire wished to join the western world. The samurai were forgotten. The ways of Bushido ignored, our lives and dedication dismissed in the New World Order."

"That's terrible," Denise Pulitzer said as she jotted in her notebook.

"It was. Many died in those first months, those that would not stand down. Many more were humiliated by the new regime, the lower caste suddenly elevated by joining the military and lording over those who once fought for them and protected their rights. Many became *Ronin*- rogue and masterless, their *Daimyos*- lords trying to hold faith to the old ways, but the Western influence proved too strong in the end and one by one they succumbed."

"Yet you hold on to those old ways?" Denise said as she paused in her notes, looking curiously at Suwan. "Even here in America. Why?"

Suwan gazed dreamily at the barren garden as she dabbed at her perspiration with a cottony towel. Diane Pulitzer knew her true past. They were true friends and confidantes. They had survived together when Death came to call, survived and grew in rituals of fire. Her daughter however simply thought of Suwan as a tutor and aide, a friend true but a fixture in the Pulitzer household beholden somehow to her mother. Too, Diane knew of Suwan's darker self, her other persona and the vow of revenge and the debt to restore her honor, and that of her father and friends, her comrades. But how much to share with Denise?

"I have *giri*," she finally said draping the towel about her neck, "Obligation. A debt owed to my family and friends that I must repay before I might find peace."

"What debt?" Denise asked, recrossing her legs and leaning forward, her pencil poised over her journal.

"My father was samurai," Suwan said as she sipped at a cold mug of tea. "He followed the ways of Bushido- the ways of honor and trained others in those ways, trying to keep them alive. He was murdered by one of his students. He and all of his followers, slain in their trust, by trickery. I survived and vowed to avenge them. I followed their killer here, from Japan to New York."

Denise's mouth curved into an 'O' as she scribbled in her journal.

"My mother was Chinese and died of the 'Black Rot' years before. Cancer. I am a half-breed and not welcome by either of my people, which is fine. I have little use for them here, seeing what they have become." Suwan dropped the towel to the side and moved towards the practice dummy again, bowing before striking a defensive pose.

"But we stray," she said as she attacked the dangling straw man, her *boken* slapping the dummy target in a wild flurry. "I cannot speak for other cultures or Medieval times, but Feudalism thrived in Japan for generations. The *daimyos* ruled their prefects. The samurai maintained order. The peasants prospered and the emperor was content, if not pleased. The land was clean, the roads secure and everyone benefited. A simpler time and way of life to be sure, but it prospered. Here in America, in your democracy there are so many without homes, work, hope."

"That's the Depression," Denise said bristling a bit. "A hard time that's affecting the whole world. In normal times…"

"Normal times are long gone," Suwan said as she slapped the straw man with her sword over and over. She screamed her rage, slashing her blade through the bundled neck of her target. The head spun and spiraled away bouncing across the snow-crusted lawn and finally rolling to a stop under the barren lilac bushes. Suwan took a deep breath, flicking her sword to the side.

"We must adjust in order to survive."

Bowing her head and shuffling her feet through slushy snow Suwan Shin*obi* humbly made her way through the crowded streets of Chinatown in lower Manhattan. She was dressed like most others, plain black, baggy cottons, quilted and layered against the chill, high-rounded collar pinned tight about her throat, cold fingers gripping the straps of the bundled bag filled with rocks and rags that she wore on her back, all for show.

The streets were packed, her people of old clogging the sidewalks bustling about in their day to day lives. Hawkers and venders lined Broadway and Canal selling their wares, shouting to be heard. Jewelry and trinkets, cloths fine and silken to coarse and ragged, incense and peppermint, sweets and tea. Children hunkered in the gutters snapping pea pods while men stood at tables gutting fish. An old woman dipped steaming rice from a bamboo pot on the corner, toothless and sallow, a penny a cup. The odors were both vulgar and intoxicating, the harsh smells of the city, of America mingling with memories of another land and time. And the noise...

Suwan tried to ignore the din, the babble of a dozen dialects merging into one mixed with broken English and smatterings of European; Irish, Italian, German and so many, many more. New York City was the melting pot as they said, the gateway to the eastern United States where so many had come and settled. It was amazing and frightening all in one.

And Suwan tried her best to blend in. She looked like them, spoke their languages but somehow she knew that they knew. She saw the sly, sideways glances, the smirks and whispers as she passed. They saw the mark; the bite of the demon *Gaki* never healed, red and tender, sometimes burning. And despite her best efforts they considered her *gaijin*, stranger and foreigner and she knew that they were right. She would never fit into their tight-knit society just as she would never belong to the world of Diane Pulitzer. She was an outsider and half-breed, but truly she did not care. Not much at any rate. She had obligation. *Giri...*

She made her way through the throng though, her eyes always roving, listening to the things they said, whispers and gossip, rumors. She followed the word, letting it lead her deeper into their world, into their midst. It was on the fringe of Chinatown where she drew up short, the corner of Essex and Avenue B.

It was called the Bank, and she supposed at one time it was. A thick, squat, square building built to mimic the larger, official government buildings just a few blocks away downtown. It was white stone with large fluted columns guarding the front entrance, high windows of stained glass and three stories of imposing edifice. But it was not the building that captured her attention.

Suwan stepped into the shadows of the building across the way, the eaves of a grocery; an old man stripping cabbage leaves eyeing her curiously. She stared across the lanes of traffic, at the long, black Lincoln and the men gathered about it. White men chatting, dressed in Stetsons and long coats, smoking cigarettes bored and nervous. Their eyes darted about giving the passing residents of Chinatown and the Lower East Side alike wide berth. Just two blocks south stood the tenements, ratchety and weathered buildings that once housed dozens per apartment with no windows at times, no running water or toilets. Roosevelt's reforms- Theodore not Franklin- were having them renovated if not demolished, but still the poor thronged to the cheap housing and lined the streets,

Jews and Irish mainly, but lately the Spanish from South America and the Caribbean, Puerto Rico.

And Suwan focused on one, his grizzled face and gaunt stance. A glint of metal she knew to be his Tommygun as he flicked his spent butt to the gutter, the tails of his woolen coat flaring wide. The lead gunsel of Boss Hoss' envoy, she was certain.

"Ai! What are you doing here? Move on!"

Suwan turned staring at the old man owner of the grocery stall. He made motions for her to leave, scowling as he waved her away.

"Please," she said in *Nihongo* bowing slightly in reverence to her elder. "I just need a moment's peace."

"You go now!" He waved her off again. Suwan scowled, pulling money from her pocket, five dollars, which she gave to the man. He eyed the money then snatched it away almost too swiftly for the eye to follow. He turned and scooped soggy rice noodles from a steaming pot into a cup and handed it to her with chopsticks. He eyed the gangsters across the way. "You get me killed." He spat and went back into his shop. Suwan forked the long noodles into her mouth turning back to the gangsters. Spicy and hot.

It was several minutes before Suwan's eyes widened. She watched as Hana and several other Orientals descended the steps of the Bank. They gathered on the sidewalk talking, eventually bowing to one another, Hana bowing the slightest she noted, he garnering the most respect apparently. Finally he turned away, lighting a cigarette as the other Orientals returned to the building. The whites came forward then, and again there was speaking she could not hear. The gangsters eventually moved back to the dark Lincoln, Hana following, his gaze drifting over the intersection finally falling on her. He grinned and flicked his cigarette away, climbing into the rear of the car, which promptly sped away.

"He is bad, that one."

Suwan jumped at the raggedy voice, turning to find the old shopkeeper standing behind her. He was smaller and thinner, ancient and with a sad look about him, in his eyes and hunched shoulders.

"He came years ago. I saw him on the streets. Evil, that one. Wormed his way into those who run the streets. The neighborhood." The old man turned and stared at her, swallowed as he glanced about. "Triad."

"Triad?" Suwan replied. "I do not understand."

"The Tong, Yakuza, the Golden Host. He is high in their ranks, much respected. Much power. Leave him be."

"I cannot," Suwan said turning back to the building. "I have obligation.

*Giri.* "

"Hrrrmmmnnn…" the old man grumbled and moved back into his shop, shaking his head. Suwan watched him go then finished her noodles and finally moved on.

"It's a gentlemen's club," Diane Pulitzer answered as they lounged in the parlor of the Pulitzer Mansion. Helga had brought them tea and sweet bread she had baked earlier in the day, a small pot of the Chai that Suwan favored, and they were relaxing along with Denise and listening to the radio playing the Jack Benny Show, a fire crackling in the hearth of the outer wall.

"They call it the Lotus Club," Diane continued nibbling at her cake. She was dressed in her sleeping gown and housecoat, both satiny lavender with slippers to match, her red hair loose about her shoulders. "Orientals only in membership, though they do host functions and invite others on occasion. I was invited some years back, a fund-raising gala for some cause they favored at the time when the club was still uptown near Madison Square. I didn't go, however. You know how I feel about those stuffy, exclusive clubs. I thought it had closed, but apparently it simply moved."

Suwan nodded knowing that Diane had always been against the segregation of the masses, whether due to race, creed, sex or monetary value. Men and women had been created in God's image, though Diane often corrected that it was His vision rather, and the Constitution declared all to be equal, though there were few that adhered to that decree. As such she hated exclusive country clubs and gentlemen societies. The latter was fading it seemed, only a few of the clubs popular at the turn of the century remaining in the city, most notably the Manhattan Club uptown in Madison Square, and apparently the Lotus Club in Chinatown.

"That your Hana is a member doesn't surprise me, and I'm sorry that I didn't think to mention it before." Diane seemed sincerely sorrowful and Suwan smiled, sipping at her tea.

"In hindsight it makes sense," Suwan said setting her cup aside and adjusting her own robe against a sudden chill. The radiator rattled in the background as it coursed with steaming water, pouring heat into the room. "I should have suspected that he would gather with the elite. And this Triad that the old man mentioned, Hana must be deeply involved there as well."

"Well, it sounds to this old news hound that Boss Horton is trying to cinch some deal with the Orientals. You saw his thugs there, so obviously there's some game going down. Maybe Hoss wants his cut, or maybe the Asians are looking to expand. Last I heard the Opium Parlors are a big trade, and I know for a fact that white men have a fancy for the Oriental women, the more exotic the better. Maybe Hoss is looking to unify the Mobs in Manhattan like Capone did in Chicago."

"I don't know." Suwan shrugged. "But I will need to get into the Lotus Club to find out. Hana may be boarding there. It could be the opportunity I have been trying to find for so long."

"I'll make some calls," Diane said as she swallowed the last of her tea and stood, stretching. "But tomorrow. Right now I'm for bed. I'm bushed." Suwan nodded.

"As am I," Suwan agreed taking up the empty teacups and placing them on the serving tray, which she lifted. "I'll leave these in the kitchen for Helga, then I am off to bed as well. I am still tired from last night's ordeal."

"I imagine you are," Diane said as she stepped towards the doorway. "Sleep tight."

"Don't let the bed bugs bite," Suwan said with a grin watching as her friend left the parlor and ascended the stairs. She pursed her lips watching Diane go, some elusive thought playing at her memory as she hefted the laden serving tray. Finally she shook her head and went away towards the kitchen, hoping that some much-needed sleep would leave her refreshed and in a better mind to sort her jumbled thoughts in the morning.

Kareta Hana descended the weathered, worn stone steps leading down into the dank dark depths beneath the lotus Club. Sconces hissing, flickering gaslight dimly lit the way as he casually stepped the stairs ignoring the water stains on the old granite walls, mold lining the base, ignoring the dank and chill. Such things had little hold or interest for him.

Finally reaching the lowest levels he paused, taking in his surroundings again as he lit a cigarette. He looked down the long corridor, at the Tong standing guard. Dozing rather, he sat in a ladder back chair tilted against the door that he was warding. He was slim and Chinese, dressed all in black quilted cotton, pants, shoes and shirt. His unruly black hair was held slightly in check by a red sash about his temples, a like strip of cloth about his waist holding his *Dao* at hand. Hana smirked at the short bladed sword as he stepped right up to the nodding guard.

Hana hooked a foot under the protruding leg of the chair and swept it out. He laughed as the guard's eyes went wide, he suddenly plummeting to the floor with a crash and a flurry of arms and legs. He ignored the warder's confused squeals and grunts and heavily placed a foot on his chest. A moment and the guard's face turned upwards, draining of blood and pale in the wavering gas lit flame.

"You are paid to sleep?" Hana said, grinning, pressing forward with his weight. The guardian winced, squirming.

"It is quiet here," the warder whined, "Dull and lonely. I could not stay awake. Forgive me, Master! It will not happen again."

"No," Hana said as he whipped his blade free with a flourish. He slashed down and across smoothly, blood gushing from the warder's throat. He flicked his blade free of blood and slid it smoothly back into its scabbard. "It will not."

Hana dragged the twitching, dying body aside and kicked the chair away before digging out his keys and unlocking the heavy oaken door before him. His nose wrinkled as he stepped beyond assaulted by the stench of unwashed humanity and feces, sweat and urine. Closing the door behind him he strode down the stone hallway.

He ignored the mewling of the captives as he came upon the first guard within, where he paused. He took a long drag from his cigarette as he looked into the closest cell, a half-naked Caucasian woman within looking haggard and ragged, hopelessness in her bleary eyes. He glanced at the guard; another Tong dressed as the other but sporting Butterfly Blades.

"Guard the door," Hana said in Mandarin and the warder bowed then rushed back along the hallway to his new position. Hana puffed on his cigarette until the outer door slammed then continued on his way.

He passed dozens of the small, barred cells each containing a straw mat and blanket, a chamber pot and nothing else beyond the resident. The resident being a woman; Negress or White, Indian or Spanish of every size and shape imaginable. Some were bound by rope and gagged, some collared and chained depending on their fire. All looked at him as he passed, eyes pleading, imploring to be set free. Hana ignored them.

They were slaves destined to be shipped to the Orient soon, most in the confining holds of *The Shiro* set to sail back to Japan before the Western New Year five days hence. Exotic and American, they would fetch a good price in the black markets of Tokyo and Shanghai, Hong Kong and Peking. The old men of the Orient would pay good money, top dollar for an American woman, and Hana would provide. And his coffers would swell and his plans would move forward, but he cared not a whit about the pathetic and prissy western women that the Triad had captured and passed them by ignoring their whining pleas for help.

He turned corners and descended a final short flight of stairs to confront another guardian before another heavy oaken door. He heard muffled whimpering coming from beyond, and the attentive guard's eyes were wide, a thin sheen of sweat lacing his skin. "Open," Hana said and the warder nodded and turned undoing the many locks.

Kareta Hana licked his lips as he stepped inside, immediately tasting the scent of bitter tang, ruddy iron of blood mingling with burning flesh. The door slammed shut behind him as he strode forward, locks slamming home as he eased into the chamber filled with a misty, roiling smoke wrought from sizzling meat, incense, smoldering coal and candles.

Hana glanced at the girl stretched upon the stone slab, her wrists and ankles bound at the four-corners. Whether Chinese or Japanese he could no longer tell as her skin had been all but flayed, her eyes gouged out. She was writhing in agony as the diminutive man sat upon the stool plied his slight sharp blade to her flesh, scraping it away. She screamed into the leather bit lashed to her mouth as the *tanto* cut into her.

"What news?" Hana asked in Mandarin as he approached, standing at the rune carved altar's edge. The withered old man looked up, his thin, chapped lips twisted in a rictus of ecstasy. He was little more than skin and bones, his pate bald, his skin pale and sickly, boiled in spots. He was dressed in gray, raggedy robes that draped his slight frame, a golden medallion hanging about his neck, laying upon his breast; a circular disk with archaic runes that even Hana did not recognize. The necromancer scraped another bit of flesh away from his sacrifice, a virgin Hana assumed as she seemed but a child. His dark eyes sparkling like black pearls in the queer light of his chamber. "What does the future hold, mage?"

"I was not scrying the future, *shushigo*, rather gathering power for thy bidding," the old man hissed not taking his eyes from the writhing form on the slab before him. His voice was thin and whistling with barely contained glee as he hunkered over the body.

Hana frowned and fished a cigarette from the slim case in his jacket pocket. Striking a Lucifer along the edge of the altar he puffed it to life, his frown turning to a smirk as the old wizard's eyes bulged at his effrontery. "I ordered information on the alliance with Horton and our Triad, its success or failure."

"Oh, that," the old man sniffed waving the thought away with a gnarled hand. "I saw into that earlier. Success, for a time at least. Your alliance will reap rewards aplenty; money, power, women."

"Good," Hana said nodding. "I do not trust Horton, but will work with him and his for my own advantage."

"There will be loss, however," the old man added, "and soon."

"Loss? What do you mean?"

The old man shrugged as he slit the girl's belly with the curved edge of his knife. She squealed into the gag back arching against the new pain as she strained at her restraints. "I do not know. That particular vein was clouded in shadow that I could not pierce. I sensed something about water, perhaps a ship."

Hana frowned again, absently watching the girl's torturous death throes as his mind considered. The only ship in any of his plans was *The Shiro*, that to transport the kidnapped women to the Orient leaving on New Year's Eve. There was much money involved, more so than associated with the opium that the vessel had delivered. As well as his pact with the warlords of the Tong and Yakuza expecting shipment of the slaves. If something went wrong, it could prove disastrous to the intricate web that he was weaving.

Hana flicked his spent butt into the coals of the brazier and strode back to the door. "Look deeper, mage. I would know more." The old man grunted behind him. "And do not take your playthings from the stock again. The women are promised, and now I must replace this one."

A wail of agony filled the chamber as Hana slid back the bolts locking the door. He paused momentarily as he opened the door, but otherwise ignored it, slamming the door behind him as he left.

"Copy Boy!"

Denise Pulitzer hurried through the bustle of the newsroom of *The World* towards the bellowing voice of Ben Marino, Ace Reporter and Columnist for the paper. She saw him at his desk hunched over his typewriter, a cloud of smoke about him as he pecked away at the keys of his old Remington, a cold cup of coffee on the corner of his desk brimming with cigarette butts. She rushed up to the desk side shifting the papers she carried under her arm to accept the copy from him that she would then hurry to the editor for approval.

Marino looked up after a moment and gave a slight smile. A cigarette dangled from his thick lips, horn-rimmed glasses with thick lenses

*The old man shrugged as he slit the girl's belly with the curved edge of his knife.*

making his eyes seem to bulge. His white collared shirt was stained with sweat along the back and under his arms, sleeves rolled to his elbows to reveal beefy forearms. Gray-haired and pushing sixty, he was a legend in New York City journalism that Denise admired with a passion.

"Ya look tired, Pulitzer," he said pausing from his work, taking a long drag from his cigarette as he eyed her up and down. In truth, she was. They had been running her ragged all morning in the newsroom since she had arrived at eight that morning for her long shift getting the Sunday evening edition ready for printing. It seemed that every reporter was on the verge of finishing some article or column and she had been at their beck and call ever since she had clocked in three hours before. Running copy to the editors and revised samples back to the reporters, photographs and negatives to the labs, getting coffee and basically slaving away for whoever called her name or title. It was exhausting, but she loved it and was very glad that her mother had suggested she take the job. Denise one day hoped to be a reporter herself, but she knew that she had to spend time in the trenches despite the fact her mother owned the newspaper.

Denise brushed a stray strand of hair from her face and took a moment to slide her feet from her heels and flex her toes. She hated that she had to dress like a Kelly Girl, in skirt, blouse and heels but she had to meet the standard. She had pulled her hair back into a tail against the blasting radiators in the newsroom, perspiration building on the back of her neck and under her own arms. "You don't even know," she said with a smile, happy for the brief respite. Marino chuckled.

"I ain't so old, kid, as I don't remember what it was like. Yer doin' fine." Denise beamed at the praise from her idol.

"Thanks!" she said cheerily, gathering his latest work and rushing off again towards the Day Editor's office. She glanced at the story that he had handed her, about the recent disappearance of women all over the city. She scanned the lines but saw that there was no real progression with the case. The police were investigating but were apparently stymied while women of every race and status were vanishing; twenty-two over the last few weeks since Thanksgiving alone. It was a real mystery and Denise was lusting to crack it.

She reached the editor's office and saw through the blinded windows that he was in a meeting with three other men, all chewing on cigarettes or cigars, smoke clouding the closed-off room despite the cracked open windows in the far wall. She moaned at her burden and kicked, thumping the door with the toe of her thick-soled pump. She saw the editor look up and motion her inside.

Denise fumbled with the door for a moment then bustled inside. The men standing in her way moved aside as she made her way to the City Desk and dropped her load on the corner looking at her boss, Harold Black. He was a portly man with thinning, graying hair and a cigarette chomping in his teeth. He raised a hand to the other men in the office–all of whom were eyeing Denise–all dressed in Stetsons and long coats and reeking of the police.

"Second drafts from the morning, Harry," Denise said with a sigh, brushing away that stray lock of hair again. Harry Black sighed himself, leaning back in his chair and rolling his cigarette to the other corner of his mouth. He thumbed through the sheaf of papers and looked up at the men.

"Inspector, I have a paper to put out and you are making that nigh impossible. If you have no more questions, I need to get back to work." Harold Black settled back into his chair and folded his arms across the girth of his belly lacing his fingers together.

"All right, Black," one of the men said slipping his hands into his coat pockets. "I want that information, though. I gotta get a Court Order ta see it, I will." The man glanced at Denise giving her an appraising scrutiny and a smirk, lust in his eyes. "I'll be back before you know it."

"I'll be here, Mulligan," Black said with a contemptuous grin. "With Diane and the lawyers. Close the door on the way out, would ya?"

The door slammed shut as the three men left and Denise sighed in relief, not quite certain why. Black was already thumbing through the papers she had brought when she turned back to him, frowning and shaking his head as he scanned a bit of copy. "What was that about?" Denise asked watching as the men moved into the elevator and finally out of sight as the operator pulled the doors closed.

"None a' your business, kid," Black said as he thumbed through the papers with a frown. "I'll call your mother later. She can tell ya if she wants. This it?" he said tapping the top of the stack of papers.

"Yes, sir, so far."

"Yeah, the day's young." Black reached for his coffee mug then frowned to see it brimming with cigarette butts. He scooped up the mug and dumped the soggy contents into his wastebasket, then handed the cup to Denise. "Get me a refill then go out and get some lunch." He dropped a Jefferson on the desktop. "Pastrami on rye with the hot mustard. George knows what I like."

"Yessir," Denise said scooping up the two-dollar bill and heading to the door.

"And whatever you want..." Black said as he leaned over the top paper, red pencil in hand slashing at misspelled words and grammatical errors, of which there appeared to be many.

"Thank you, Mister Black," Denise said as she hurried from the office and through the bustling newsroom, her heels clacking in her wake on the linoleum tiled floor.

It was not yet noon of the following day as Suwan accompanied Diane down the several short flights of stairs to the sub-basement of the *New York World* building. Both women were dressed against the bitter cold outside, scarves and hats and long woolen coats over their business apparel. Though the sun was out and shining brilliantly the temperature had taken a nosedive and was barely in the double-digits. The weather of course did little to deter the hustle and bustle of downtown Manhattan, the packed icy streets mobbed with the denizens of Newspaper Row and the government buildings not so far away. But then it was the same in any part of the city on a normal weekday of business.

"I really hate coming down here," Diane Pulitzer groused as she stepped to the final landing, four floors beneath street level. "It's always so damn cold, but in winter it's like an ice box." Suwan nodded and stepped to the landing as Diane opened the fire door, the breath of both women misting in the chill air. Beyond the opening she saw a dim and dingy hallway stretching away to the right and left.

"But they have to keep it cool and dry to preserve the papers," Diane continued turning to the right, her heels clicking on the tiled floor with her brisk pace. "Especially in the summer. If the humidity got to the old newsprint, they'd be ruined. At least that's what Bones says. Personally I think he's just part penguin and likes it cold."

Suwan Shin*obi* laughed lightly as she followed her friend down the long hallway, turning at the end to the right and finally coming to their destination: the Morgue, or at least its main office. Suwan knew that the entire basement floor stored mainly preserved copies of old issues of the *World*, since its founding in 1890 by Diane's father. According to Diane however, in the many storage rooms were also maps of all sort, building blueprints, all manner of books and legal doctrines and even copies of other newspapers from around the world. According to Diane the man in charge of the Morgue, Vincent 'Bones' Bonner was something of an information packrat.

As promised Diane had started making calls early that morning as the workday had begun to help Suwan get into the Lotus Club. She had started with the club itself, but had quickly been stymied as the phone operator had told her that the club was closed to visitors for the indefinite future. Diane had considered bribing her way through the front door but Suwan had nixed that idea, knowing that Hana would have given her description and probably Diane's as well, if he was indeed a high-ranking member of the club. Unperturbed Diane called the city offices of buildings and houses, calling in a favor with a worker there to see the blueprints of the building, perhaps to find a more secretive way in. The city worker had called back some twenty minutes later stating that they had no plans for the building on file, apparently they had been lost in a fire some years prior.

"How convenient," Diane had said lighting a cigarette with her Zippo and snapping the lid closed with an audible clack. She had leaned back in her chair still dressed in her housecoat tapping the metal lighter against the tabletop as Helga bustled about the table clearing the breakfast dishes, the older woman huffing and puffing as she worked.

"Seems someone at the club is not stupid, covering their tracks maybe? The fire could be coincidence, but why don't I think so?" Diane puffed on her cigarette and Suwan knew that she was deep in thought, her mind probably awhirl with ideas.

"Perhaps it was," Suwan commented taking a sip of her cooling morning tea, "but where does that leave us? I will simply have to break into the club."

"Oh, I'm not done yet," Diane said sitting forward in her chair and picking up the telephone receiver, dialing a number on the rotary. "I have one more call to make. One I should have made first." Suwan heard the clacking sound of the phone ringing on the line, finally, abruptly halting as someone picked up on the other end.

"This is Pulitzer," Diane said tapping ash from her cigarette. "Get me the Morgue."

"Hullo, Miz Pulitzer," the old man within said as Suwan followed Diane into the cluttered office. It was crowded and claustrophobic, filled with stacks of newsprint and papers and smelling of mold, must and cigarette smoke. There was a desk overloaded with newspapers, three chairs and an empty water cooler against one wall, filing cabinets lining another. Suwan noted framed newspaper front pages on the mildewed walls proclaiming the Spanish-American War, Admiral Dewey's celebration parade, the announcement of The Great War and more recently the Stock Market Crash.

"Hello, Bones," Diane said dropping into one of the chairs before the desk. "How are you?"

The old Black man smiled a yellow-toothed smile and bobbed his head. Suwan figured him to be in his seventies at least with a thin frame and wispy hair about the edges of his head. His eyes were a sharp brown though and seemed sparkling with intelligence. "I'm fine, Miz," he said coming from behind the desk to shake Diane's hand, then glancing at Suwan.

"My confidant," Diane provided, "and my friend, Suwan."

"Pleased," the man said shaking Suwan's hand as she bowed in respect. "My honor."

"So, what did you find, Bones?" Diane said getting to the point after the pleasantries were over. "Tell me something good. Figured if anyone would have the skinny on the Lotus Club it would be you." The old man grinned and hustled behind his desk again.

"Found a blueprint of the building," he said almost gushing as he spread a large sheet of vellum across his desk. "It's old though, an' they probably done renovations since these. Almost thirty years, but…" Bones grabbed another sheaf of blueprints from a stack on the floor and dropped it onto the desk. "What I got's here is even better.

"Seems the old Pneumatic Subway had a tunnel runnin' under Houston Street across the island from the East River to the Hudson." Both Diane and Suwan leaned in to peer at the map and where the man was tapping a bony finger. "Just a block away from your Lotus Club."

"I thought the Pneumatic Subway was a myth," Diane said looking up at the beaming old man. "I remember some crackpot wanting to fund its building back in the 1800's, but I thought it got shelved."

"Every myth in this city comes from a fact, Miz," the man said with authority. "It was built back in the 1840's an' didn't even last ten years. The tunnel was closed up an' forgotten, but it's still there. And it's connected with the sewers," Bones said as he unrolled another map across his desk. "There's probably locked doors all along the route, but figure once past those, ya walk a couple blocks a tunnels an' yer in."

"Locked doors are not a problem," Suwan offered peering at the ancient maps, "but how do I initially get in? Where, I mean?" She looked up at the old man to find him grinning widely.

"The city's digging for one a' their new Independent lines, cuttin' right across East Houston. They're rippin' out the old Trolley tracks on Broadway too. Streets are so busted up you can't help but fall into the sewers. From there it's just a short hike east and downtown and you're there." Bones tapped a long fingernail to the map, smiling widely, which caused Suwan to smile in return.

"May I copy these?" she asked hopefully. Bones smirked and turned to his desk, rifling through the reams of papers piled there.

"No need, Missy," he said as he pulled a sheet of typing paper from a stack and handed it to her. "Already done."

Suwan took the sheet and scrutinized it, Diane peering over her shoulder. Rough, jagged lines etched onto the stark white paper indicating the sewers and the forgotten subway tunnel scribbled words and directions marking the way. Suwan looked up smiling and bowed to the man.

"I thank you," she said bowing to her elder with appreciation and respect.

"Bones, you're a wonder," Diane added stepping to the desk. She leaned in and kissed the old man on the cheek as she rested her hands on the blotter for support. When she stepped away again there was a Jackson Note on the desktop. "You ought'a put your money in your wallet, Vincent, before it gets lost in this jumble."

Vincent 'Bones' Bonner nodded his head with a grin and snatched up the double sawbuck, slipping the twenty into his baggy pants pocket. "I will, Miz Pulitzer, an' thankee."

New Year's Eve

"You're certain about this?" Diane Pulitzer asked her yet again, her breath billowing plumes of wispy mist despite the heater's blasting warmth there in the back of the publisher's Nash Ambassador. The weather had taken another dive, frigid Canadian air swooping down from the north and blowing across the Great Lakes. The radio threatened snow, quite possibly a blizzard striking as Manhattan celebrated the turning of the year. Diane and Suwan both had dressed for the arctic blast in gloves, long woolen coats and thick sweaters beneath, but both still felt the cold seeping into their bones.

Suwan sighed, looking to her friend seated beside her in the back of the long, black car seeing that expression of concern that she had seen so many times before over the years. Suwan *Shinobi*, lips tight and thin nodded sharply.

"You confirmed my contact's tip yourself, Diane. *The Shiro* sails for the Orient tonight with the high tide not long after midnight. Whatever Hana's schemes, they bear fruit tonight." Suwan forced a smile. "It's now or never."

Suwan saw her friend sigh, worry lines creasing her otherwise smooth skin about her lips and eyes. Even after all these years, Diane was not comfortable with Suwan's role of the vigilante, a "masked man" ignoring the laws and police and taking justice into her own hands. She understood, but did not like it.

But when "Old Rog" had found her and told her that the *Shiro* was scheduled to slip away in the dark of night, she knew that she had to act. In truth she had been planning on sneaking into the Lotus Club this night anyway. She had been practicing harder than ever for the past few days, honing her skills in stealth and sword, her abilities with *shuriken*, the throwing stars favored by *ninja* assassins. Too, her *katana* shattered by the demon she trained with her *wakizashi*, the Japanese short sword, companion to the longer *katana*. She had searched Chinatown for a replacement to her broken blade, but if one existed the denizens of that district were not willing to sell to her, the outcast.

And so she had trained; in the cold and dark and the glare of high noon when the beaming sun made the icy snow sparkle with dazzling brilliance. She practiced in the misty morning, damp fog licking about her boots, slashing her *boken* at the straw man, throwing razor sharp stars into her target. She stretched and lifted weights, climbed sheer walls and did acrobatics, tumbling, trying to prepare for any contingency that might arise. But she knew of course that when the battle was joined all planning was but a whim and forgotten.

"I wish you'd simply call in the police," Diane said biting her lip as she looked out into the swirling snow just drifting down. It was light yet, but the flakes were getting bigger and moist already dusting the recently cleared streets with a fresh, slick layer of white. "We can call in a report of a Speak Easy, or even a fire. That'd give the boys in blue reason to bust the joint and throw a monkey wrench in Hana's plans."

"You know I can't, Diane" Suwan said with a shake of her head as she sloughed out of her thick longcoat. She had forgone her traditional kimono for more practical clothes against the cold. She wore long johns beneath her body suit; not attractive but functional. Her riding boots of course with a *tanto* slid into an inner sheath, bracers on her arms and a thick, hooded sweater over a padded tunic belted with her *obi*. Her *boken* and *wakizashi* were slipped through her belt, two leather pouches suspended as well, one containing her *shuriken*, the other caltrops. She knew that her father would be displeased with her tactics, following the ways of the assassin rather than the knight, but Hana had to be stopped, her comrades and family avenged.

"It is a matter of honor. I must redeem myself and avenge my fellows... my father."

"I know," Diane sighed as she put a cigarette to her lips, lighting it with a flick of her silver Zippo. She exhaled and Suwan could feel the woman's torment. Her friend was worried for her, and that in its way gave her strength.

"We're here," Lancaster the driver said as he eased the Nash to the slush at the curb, shifting the car to neutral to idle. Suwan forced a smile, meeting his gaze in the rearview mirror, noting concern in his eyes as well. "I can go with you Miss, if you like."

Suwan stared at the big man driving the car. He was well over six feet tall and thickly muscled, in his forties and a veteran of the Great War. She suspected that he knew how to fight, and she was touched at his offer but again she shook her head no.

"Thank you, no. I must do this myself."

"We'll wait nearer the club," Diane said while puffing on her cigarette. "We'll be ready, should you need us." Suwan smiled, gripping her friend's arm and giving it a loving squeeze. She nodded her head, her throat too raw with emotion to speak, opened the door and slipped out into the frigid darkness...

"Thanks, Otto! I owe ya one."

Denise Pulitzer jumped as Ben Marino slammed the telephone receiver into its cradle. He had that look in his eyes as he stumped a cigarette butt into the over-flowing ashtray on the corner of his desk and stood, slipping into his jacket. He gathered pen and pad and hustled towards the door to the City Room, not five steps as he lit another cigarette.

"What is it?" Denise asked rushing up beside him, a ream of files snuggled to her breast. Her eyes were wild with excitement, knowing that Marino had just gotten some lead on a huge story.

"The missing women," Marino said as he grabbed his longcoat and hat from the pegs by the door, shoving his arms into the sleeves. He wrapped a scarf about his throat. "Seems they're gonna be shipped out of the country tonight. Some white slavery ring. I gotta get downtown, ASAP."

"Let me come with you!" Denise begged following her idol into the hall where he waited impatiently for the elevator. "I can help!"

Marino smirked, looking the Pulitzer girl up and down. "Ya got moxy, kid, but it's too dangerous. Yer mother would fire me, after she killed me."

"Please, Ben!" Denise whined watching the arrow above the elevator doors as it neared their floor. "I'll never be a reporter if I don't get a break. My mother won't let me even try!"

Marino stared at the girl, remembering the mother years past. Finally smiling he turned towards the elevator doors as a soft bell chimed. "You know yer way around a camera, kid?"

"Yes!" Denise shouted almost squealing with excitement.

"Get one and meet me in the lobby. Five minutes or you get left behind. I'll flag a cab." Marino stepped into the empty elevator car even as Denise pumped a fist in triumph. She hurried off to find a camera…

Kiri dropped the last few feet to the slight, slimy ledge running the length of the old, abandoned Pneumatic Subway tunnel. It was dank but surprisingly lit, gaslight sconces flickering along the rounded walls and disappearing into the distance, east and west. The sewer smell was thick and a thin mist roiled along the surface of the slow-moving water. Rats ran the ledge scurrying past her feet, old archaic terrors rising up in prenatal memory.

She had made her way easily into the sewers, heaving open a heavy manhole cover and climbing the metal ladder down into the depths. She had searched through the muck and mire for a few minutes, finally finding the sealed doors into the abandoned subway line right where Bones had said they would be. It was a simple matter to open the locked doors and make her way within, using slim rod and wire to pick ancient locks holding the binding chains. She had walked the short flight of slick stone steps to the edge of an opening, the rotting remains of a fallen dock jutting from the waters a few feet away. She stood on the walkway now getting her bearings looking east and west, knowing that the Lotus Club was just a block to the south. She saw an opening on the far side of the water not unlike her own, a rotting dock before a set of stairs though in better shape than her own at a glance.

She heard a crack of leather whip accompanied by muffled whimpers to her right…

To the east the tunnel appeared empty, but to the west she saw flickering shadows cast in the gaslight several blocks away fluttering over the tiled walls in a strange dance. A large group making their way down the tunnel towards whatever exit existed on the West Side and the Hudson River. Kiri followed the shadows and the sounds, easing slowly and quietly along the slime-coated ledge.

Within a few yards she was close enough to make out the shadowy group. Men; Orientals dressed in black and red, huddled against the bitter cold herding over a dozen women along the tunnel's walkway on the far side of the tube. The women were white mostly as far as she could tell, scantily clad and some even naked, all bound and gagged, leashed together in a long line. The men sported various weapons, swords and guns mainly as they urged their charges onward, interspersed amongst the captives. A small boat rode the waters, two men poling the channel, two others bearing rifles trained on their charges.

Kiri stared long at the group, then glanced back at the side opening back to the east farther along the tunnel that she knew led eventually into the bowels of the Lotus Club, and Hana. She sighed, gripping her *boken* tighter, wringing the hilt in her hands.

She cursed, hissing under her breath and hurried down the tunnel to the west.

"Stay behind me, kid," Ben Marino hissed as he eased along the old docks of the Bull Shipping Lines at Pier Thirty-Nine. Denise nodded, clutching her Hansa Canon to her chest, checking the security of the neck strap for the hundredth time since the harrowing drive from uptown. She licked her lips and tugged her scarf up against the bitter cold, dressed in her own longcoat but cursing her pencil skirt and platform heels every step of the way.

She worried that the 35 mm would not work in the arctic-like air, but Marino had assured her that it would be fine as the yellow cab had surged almost haphazardly through the snowy streets, running lights and ignoring restrictions as the cabby had been promised a Lincoln to get them downtown ASAP. Denise had clutched at the armrest as the hack slid around corners, horn blaring as it roared through stoplights at breakneck speed. She was as pale as a ghost and shivering with sweat when the cab finally skidded to a stop along the West Side Highway. Marino tossed the cabby his fare and the five and bolted into the cold, Denise hot on his heels.

"There…" Marino whispered as he crouched in the shadows of a warehouse at the edge of the docks pointing to a ship at berth at the pier. "Get a picture," he said pointing at the old freighter. Denise complied, though she doubted it would be any good without a flash and from the distance in the darkness. "The *Shiro*," he said, jotting notes in his journal. "Nip ship, probably hauling contraband for the war effort. In this case, women. I hear there's a big demand for blond hair and blue eyes in the Orient these days."

"Japan's not at war," Denise said taking two more photos, hoping one at least would come out. Marino glanced back at her and smirked, blowing into his cold hands.

"In this business, kid, ya gotta learn to read between the lines. Japan's all smiles right now, but mark my words, there's a lot of land in China and South Asia they'd love to call their own. Oil, coal, metals; it's an untapped wellspring of money just waiting to be taken. They hook up with Hitler and they get what they want, eventually." Marino continued to peer through the swirling snow at the docked ship, his eyes scanning the piers as well as the decks. Denise could see a few crewmen aboard the ship, fewer still along the docks, all idle as though waiting.

"It's quiet," Denise said finally realizing. "Too quiet. I haven't been to the wharves often, but even the Staten Island and Jersey ferries are bustling with activity no matter the hour."

Marino turned back and smiled. "Good eye, kid. That was my tip. Otto's the dock foreman for the Bull Line on the graveyard. Told me he was paid a tidy sum of money to give the workers the night off. A very tidy sum."

"Look!" Denise hissed pointing at the ship in dock even as shadowy figures started to appear in the distance. They were bundled against the cold but dressed in black with streaks of scarlet; belts and headbands. Several scrambling up onto the pier from a ladder that dipped down over the bank of the river. Denise's eyes went wide as she saw several scantily clad, bound and gagged women follow, herded up the ladder from the river, grouped and urged towards the ship's gangway one by one to gather before the plank. The men had guns and other more archaic weapons, swords and poles that she could see. A jet black Lincoln rolled up along the street even as the women were shoved along, prodded by sticks and even a short

*"It's quiet," Denise said, finally realizing. "Too quiet."*

whip wielded by one man.

"Here now, what's this?" Marino said easing forward, scampering along the wall in a low crouch, Denise following as best she could.

Four men piled from the Lincoln bundled against the cold, as was everyone, save the women. These four Denise saw were white and swarthy looking in longcoats and wide-brimmed hats pulled low. Two, she saw were carrying Tommy-guns, one a sawed-off shotgun, the fourth having his hands stuffed deeply in his coat pockets.

"Get that!" Marino hissed still scrabbling closer and Denise paused to click off several photos hoping one would take in the dim. She saw a man step to the top of the gangway then, Asian as near as she could tell. He seemed ignorant of the cold, wearing a fine suit and long woolen coat that was open and flapping in the wind, his hair blowing wildly. He paused at the railing, leaning forward as he surveyed the scene below.

"Get them aboard," he finally said his voice deep as he shouted over the howl of the wind. Denise saw the men start to prod the captive women again, herding them towards the gangway.

"That's 'Goose' Gideon," Marino whispered indicating the lead white man. "Boss Hoss' main gunsel. He's got a nose infection, honks when he blows." Marino shrugged even as something along the docks drew everyone's attention. Guns were raised and the women froze; the first in line poised on the gangway. Denise could not see for the snow and the dark but gasped as men screamed, shrill, piercing howls of agony cutting through the night.

They had reached the end of the tunnel; the women herded into a cloistered group as the small ship thumped up against a huge metal grate that locked the tube away. The men kept their weapons trained on the women as one on the walkway unlocked a barred metal door. There were rotting docks on both sides of the tunnel, stairways blocked and loaded with debris; apparently once a boarding point for the West Side of the old pneumatic subway. Kiri cursed under her breath and eased silently forward in the fluttering gaslight, edging along the slime encrusted wall.

She could see in the distance a similar barred gate on her side of the tunnel, along with a docking area of old, rotting wood. She would either have to pick the locks on the gate of her side to continue following, or swim the frigid waters of the tunnel to get out. She watched as the men disembarked the small skiff, the guards ushering the captive women out of the tube and apparently up onto the Hudson Docks by the age worn stairs.

As the last of the guards made his way up the old, abandoned steps she hurried forward to inspect the lock on her door on her side. She smirked at the simple lock and withdrew thin but stout wires from an inner pocket on her belt; an easy pick. Within moments the tumblers fell into place, the rusting lock popping open and she was hurrying up the slimy, icy stairs on her side of the ancient, forgotten docking station.

The storm had increased in intensity during her time down in the sewers and tunnels. The wind was whipping and more, larger flakes of wet snow flung through the darkness. She could barely see the chunks of ice floating in the Hudson just a few yards away as she carefully stepped out onto what was left of the old pier; the boarding area of the pneumatic subway. Rotting wood groaned underfoot as she made her way to the access ladder, the old stairs outside long since removed, and up staying close to the retaining wall and listening to the sounds just overhead.

As the voices moved away, *wakizashi* in hand now, *boken* sheathed she gripped the icy iron rungs of the ladder and climbed high enough to see the scene above. The guards were urging the women towards the ship, The *Shiro*, whipping and prodding cruelly. There were others on the docks, more Orientals bearing the red headband of the Triad, all armed. Too, she saw the white man that she had seen nights before and three others, the men of Boss Horton's employ. In all almost two dozen men that she could see, all armed and dangerous, ready to kill.

Kiri silently pulled herself up onto the wharves and dipped into her pouch of *shuriken*. She fingered four throwing stars and ran forward, flinging the deadly metal blades in a wide arch. She heard screams as she charged forward into the storm, her *wakizashi* biting deeply as she passed into the foe, tasting blood.

Kareta Hana had been watching the captive women being herded towards the ship's gangway when he had heard the first screams even though he was yards above the wharf, and over the whistling winds. He glanced sharply to his right, eyes squinting into the blowing snow and scanning the docks for the source of the screams, and whatever had caused them. Though in his dark heart he knew the reason, and whom he would see.

Three of the Triad's hirelings lay on the docks, two unmoving while the third thrashed about clutching at his throat. A fourth was teetering on his knees, his hand pressing to his opposite shoulder. Even from his distance he could smell the blood and licked his lips with a grin.

A flurry of movement and his gaze shifted, sweeping over the Triad's men and Hoss' lackeys. They were slow to respond to the fury in their midst, only now raising their weapons in more a panic than the trained efficiency that he had been assured were their stock in trade. Hana saw a spray of blood as an arm, hand still gripping a sword spiraled away, another man falling before the blade hit the docks with a resounding CLANG!

And then he saw her.

She was poetry in motion, dancing an intricate ballet that few could ever master, weaving through the startled "warriors" with the grace of a panther and just as savage. Hana watched almost mesmerized as she slipped through the mob, his defenders, touching and as untouchable as the mist that she had named herself after. "Kiri," he whispered a smile lighting his face.

Kareta Hana reached within the folds of his longcoat and drew the blade, the sword envisioned, forged and created by Masamune centuries before. The blade he had stolen from Suwan Shinobi's dead father and teacher. He held the blade before him for a moment, vertical and rigid, staring hard as light glinted off of the fine metal, then abruptly slashed to the right in a wide arc; saluting she who was about to die.

Kareta Hana leapt over the ship's rail with a savage cry, plummeting to the docks far below.

Kiri slashed, the *wakizashi* pausing only slightly as it was impeded, biting into flesh. She ignored the startled cry of pain, withdrawing the blade as she swept forward, ignoring the body that toppled in her wake as she brought up the *boken* to block with her left arm. She slammed away the *sai* with a flick and twirl of her wrist, the short sword in the grip of her right hand biting deeply into the exposed belly of her foe.

She ignored the blood, the sudden stench of fecal matter as the dying body expelled its waste, flipping high and over the latest to bar her path. She lashed out in mid-flight, her sword arcing down to slice through another of the black-garbed assailants. She landed in a crouch, rolling and cutting, a shrill screech as a leg was severed at the ankle, another man falling to the rotting wood.

Lightniing flared and thunder erupted as she scrambled to her feet, dashing into the remainder of the disarrayed mob. Bullets ripped at the wharf, wood chips flying at her heels as more men screamed, her enemy slaying one another. She slipped her *boken* under her arm and dipped her hand into the *shuriken* pouch again. She drew the razor sharp stars and threw towards the flickering light of the Tommy-guns, the black-garbed Orientals scattering before her and the hail of ripping bullets. She was rewarded with two piercing screams echoing in harmony as she gripped the wooden practice sword again, still striving forward.

Kiri could see the women huddled near the gangway of the ship, their faces ashen, filled with fear, eyes wide over their gags. They were forgotten for the moment, which was good, as soon the surprise of her assault would be over and those yet remaining would rally to focus. But there was still time, heartbeats perhaps, and in that time two more fell to her blades.

And then Hana was before her.

He was handsome, the wind blowing at his coat, his raven black hair whipping wildly. He held her father's sword almost casually at his side, a grin creasing his dark features. His brown eyes flicked to her side even as she heard the footfalls. She whipped the *wakizashi* up in a flourish and back, driving the blade through the gullet of the assassin creeping up noisily from behind. Hana laughed.

"I am impressed, little Mist," Hana said, chuckling, actually bowing his head in the slightest respect. "You have grown. I was not so sure after our last encounter, but I know you were caught up in the battle rage and blood lust, letting your emotions guide you. I- NO!"

Kiri spun, the short sword slicing deeply through the throat of another in a wide arc. Her assassin dropped to his knees, his spear clattering on the wooden docks as he fell forward, dead.

"She is mine!" Hana shouted, whipping his blade about in *kata*, finally poised and posing, ready to attack or defend. He smirked. "Shall we dance?"

As if on cue a gunshot exploded into the night and Kiri lunged forward.

"What're we gonna do, Goose?" Carney asked his eyes wide as he watched the melee unfolding just a few yards away. "I mean… that Chinee frail's cuttin' the boss' business partners ta ribbons. Ain't never seen the like."

Goose Gideon had to agree, watching as the slip of a girl cut through the Triad's men, Hana's guards. He could not tell for certain, but he was pretty sure that it was the same girl from the docks uptown a few nights back. The one that Hana had dumped into the Hudson. Gideon wondered briefly what her grief with Hana was, then figured it was none of his concern.

What *did* concern him was the deal that Boss Hoss had made with Hana and his Asian cronies. It hadn't been easy gathering the dozen odd women that were part of the deal's seal. Couldn't just round up some whores, no. The Orientals had wanted clean women, women of culture and erudite. Goose snorted, honking slightly, puffing on the cigarette dangling in between his lips. Lucky they didn't want virgins, he supposed.

He saw Hana leap over the ship's rail, the man's war cry drawing his attention. He boggled at the jump, arcing out and landing easily in a crouch on the old docks; thirty feet at least from the ship to the wharf. Shaking his head and flicking his cigarette butt into the storm he drew his Luger from the shoulder holster under his coat.

He fired one quick shot, putting a bullet into the brow of one of the Orientals, panic in the man's eyes as he fled from the battle. The man buckled almost folding in half and dead before he hit the snow-slicked wood. Goose glanced at the man briefly, eyes wide and steam swirling up from the blood swollen hole in his forehead, then looked back to the battle.

"Kill the bitch," he said raising his handgun again, trying to get a bead on the girl.

"But... we'll kill Hana's men!" Carney squealed and Goose really wanted to plug the stooge right then, but he held back.

"They're Chinks, Carney," Goose grumbled as the girl flitted in and out of sight. "There's a billion more where these came from. Fry 'em!"

Goose saw Carney glance at Kramden, the portly thug shrugging and locking and ratcheting his machine gun. Both men raised their chatter guns and opened fire, spraying the crowd. The Asians screamed and scattered, the two gunsels spattering the docks first then raking the mob. Screams rose up over the wind as men were hit, wounded, dying... dead. Gideon did not care, aiming on the girl.

He blinked as she spun however, her arm flung outstretched and winced in pain as something slammed into his shoulder. He glanced down and saw blood seeping into the material of his longcoat, a slim cut in the fabric. He heard the clatter of metal bouncing on the docks and looked over to see Kramden and the fourth of their quartet, Allston, lying dead on the ground, blood spurting from their throats. He looked closer and saw thin, metallic star shapes protruding from their bloody wounds.

He turned at the sound of Hana's voice shouting over the melee and saw the Asian gang lord squaring off against the girl. Hana seemed to be smiling, laughing and Gideon had to wonder if the man wasn't just a bit looney tunes.

"Goose!" Carney shrieked suddenly in his face, the gunsel's eyes wide as he waved at the two dead bodies at their feet. "She... She killed Kramden! Allston! What... What..."

Goose Gideon raised his Luger and planted a slug in Carney's eye. Gray matter spewed from the back of the man's head even as he crumpled to the ground. Gideon stared at the dead body as he plucked the *shuriken* from his shoulder, turning it over in his fingers before tossing it aside.

He looked back to the battle, watching as Hana and the girl fought with their swords. He looked to the ship and saw the crew scrambling about making ready to get under way. There were maybe five or six of the Triad's men still on their feet and ready to help Hana. Goose Gideon weighed his options.

"Screw this," he said to himself, holstering his gun and climbing back into the Lincoln. Skidding tires and rubber burning he sped off into the storm, cutting his losses.

"Oh my god!" Denise Pulitzer screamed frantic and frenzied as she stared at the carnage unfolding on the docks not so far away. Men were dying- horribly- as some woman with a sword waded through their ranks, cutting them down like a farmer scything wheat. She had never seen the like before, and hoped to God she never would again.

"Denise!"

Denise Pulitzer shuddered pulled from her shock by Ben Marino's voice shouting at her. He was crouching next to a stack of packing crates on a wooden pallet ready to be loaded aboard some ship. Even as he stared at her she could see that he was jotting into his notepad, scribbling shorthand without even looking.

"Take pictures, dammit!" he shouted glancing back at the fight, then back to her. "We'll get a Pulitzer for this!" he said, looking at her oddly for a moment before finally shrugging and scurrying closer to the battle. Denise chewed on her lower lip, screwed up her courage and followed suit, winding her camera ahead as she skidded to a crouch behind her mentor.

Denise scanned the battle, looking for the shot. There were not many of the black-garbed men left standing, and the woman with the sword was facing off with the man, his own longer sword held on high. She saw the ship's crew bustling on deck, getting ready to cast off she imagined. The captive women still stood, petrified before the gangway. She raised the camera, her eye in the viewfinder.

Denise took the photos: the terrified, kidnapped women, the ship and its crew, the men clad in black and scarlet, the dead. She heard a car roar away but did not turn as she focused on the two that seemed to be the center of the melee. She rotated the lens, trying to bring the pair into clarity and suddenly gasped.

"Suwan?" she whispered lowering the camera even as her mother's friend and confidant and the man clashed swords.

Kiri struck first.

Breathing hard already from fighting Hana's minions, chilled from the icy winds and damp from the huge wet flakes of snow swirling about her, still she fought. Though the need for vengeance burned in her breast she kept her anger in check, her emotions in rein. She eyed the *Gaki* warily, knowing that the demon was dangerous and devious, and especially skilled with the master *katana* he wielded. Still she struck; three flashing blows to neck, hip and thigh respectively. Hana countered easily, as expected, almost casually and one-handed.

But her initial assault was a feint, the last strike designed to let momentum carry her spinning. She lashed out with a low kick driving the heel of her boot into Hana's right knee. She was rewarded with the muffled crack of bone and a wince of pain wiping the smile from her opponent's lips.

Hana staggered back a bit, favoring the leg that should have been broken with a slight limp. Kiri knew however that the demon healed quickly and so pressed her advantage stepping through her spin with *wakizashi* outstretched to slash at Hana's midsection, but the *Gaki*'s blade was there to parry angling the blow up and away. Kiri stepped back to first position ready to attack or defend as Hana's mocking grin returned.

"Very nice, Suwan-Chan. You are truly beautiful in your skill when you do not allow emotion to rule your actions." Kiri ground her teeth at the insult, calling her a little girl with his hollow praise. He chuckled. "If I were not what I am, your *shushigo*, master and better I would already be defeated."

Kiri started to retort but Hana looked away, shouting in Mandarin

Chinese, "Get the women on the ship, fools! Tell Inzo to get underway." He turned back to Kiri then and gripped his *katana* in both hands. "This won't take long."

"Dammit!"

Denise Pulitzer looked up from pawing through the camera case slung across her shoulder, her hands coming up empty in her quest for another roll of film, wondering why Marino was cursing. She followed his gaze and saw that the remaining half dozen Orientals were racing towards the captive women even as men from the ship were pounding down the gangway. The women were just standing there like sheep, though apparently the men had snapped from their startlement, Suwan wading through their ranks like Death unbound.

"They're taking the women," Ben Marino said glancing back. "The woman with the sword's not going to be able to help." Denise saw frustration in her mentor's eyes, his hands clenched in fists.

A clangor of clashing steel on steel stole Denise's attention and she saw now that the Asian man was pressing his attack. His sword seemed almost invisible with the speed of his assault, whipping about in a flurry that Suwan was hard-pressed to counter. Every blow seemed to force her back as she sought to defend herself, blocking every strike. Denise gasped as a blow slipped through her friend's defenses, slicing deeply into the padded jacket she wore, Suwan wincing in obvious pain.

But then Suwan lashed out, her own blade swooping down to slash the man's shoulder, he in turn hissing at the wound. The two separated again, steam rising in the chill as both heaved for breath, swords raised as they considered one another.

"Ben..."

Denise Pulitzer yelped, jumping as the explosive roar of gunfire erupted in the night. Immediately she saw Ben Marino running towards the black-garbed Asian men, a discarded Tommy gun in hand and firing wildly into their ranks. She saw three spin and fall as he swept his aim upwards, two more on the ship's gangway staggering to fall over the railing and into the icy waters of the Hudson. The women were screaming in muffled terror and Denise saw that one was on her knees wailing into her gag, blood running down her bare arm.

The remaining men on the gangway ran back up onto the ship while others already at the rails opened fire with guns of their own. She watched as Marino stopped, raised his gun and raked the ship's deck sending the crew scattering. He then swept the spray of bullets back to the men on the docks, even now charging towards him. Two more fell before the raggedy roar of gunfire ceased, the gun's drum magazine empty. She watched as Marino pulled at the trigger uselessly, then gasped.

"Ben!" she shouted even as the last of the Orientals cast his short spear. She watched in horror as Marino looked up, the spear slamming into his chest. He staggered backwards, the useless gun falling from his grip to clatter upon the docks, his body tumbling down after just a moment later. He squirmed a bit, kicking, then lay still.

"No!" Denise shouted running forward throwing caution to the wind.

"I am surrounded by idiots," Hana said as he turned back to Kiri, "and would-be heroes."

Kiri was breathing hard, every breath shooting a lance of pain through her chest from Hana's cut. She knew that she was bleeding, exhausted and aching but she held her stance waiting for the *Gaki*'s next move. Hana in turn seemed unimpeded by his wounds; the scar on his shoulder unblemished, his leg undisturbed. He stared at her, no longer grinning, then glanced at the women as a shout came down from the ship.

The women were finally moving away from the ship, running for the safety of the city. Kiri saw men on the *Shiro* casting off docking lines even as the engines roared churning water in the stern. The last of the black-garbed Orientals stood just a few yards away unsure of what to do, an old white man lying at his feet, a short spear jutting from his chest.

"Fools all," Hana said shaking his head then focusing on Kiri. "This ends now," he said raising his blade "You were an amusement for a time, little Mist, but now you are a distraction that I need to eliminate, if I am to achieve my goals. Time to die…"

"Stop!"

Hana actually paused, both he and Suwan looking to the source of the shrieking voice. Kiri's eyes went wide to see Denise Pulitzer holding a sawed-off shotgun leveled at Hana's chest. The gun was wavering, and Kiri could see panic and tears in her friend's eyes. She heard Hana laugh.

"You must be joking, child," Hana said, his sword still between him and Kiri. "You can barely lift that, let alone aim or fire. Put it down and walk away, little girl." Hana started towards Denise.

"Shoot!" Kiri shouted even as she started forward as well, her blade held vertical, arcing back.

Hana swung around, slicing low as Kiri swung high. Hana cursed as her blade bit into his arm, his own sword slashing into her at almost the same spot as her previous wound.

BOOM!

Hana sprawled backwards to fall to the docks with the force of the buckshot. Kiri squealed in pain too; the wide spray of the shot biting into her hip and thigh. She heard a scream as she fell though and saw Denise flying backwards as well, staggering on her fashionable heels to drop over the edge of the docks.

"No!" she cried, lunging forward seeing the hand clutching the edge of the wharf, sprawling herself as pain wracked her side. She fell, skidding on the slick, rotting wood. She scrambled forward crawling on hands and knees to find Denise dangling precariously from the docks, the frigid waters of the Hudson River just a few feet below her kicking legs. Denise's face was awash in panic, her mouth wide in a silent scream. Kiri knew that if her friend fell she would not survive the icy plunge and she reached out to grab the girl's wrist.

"This round to you, little Mist," she heard Hana say, glancing back over her shoulder even as she clutched at the wrist of her confidant's daughter. Hana was on his feet, sword in hand and looking to the east. She heard sirens blaring, some distance away. Hana sighed then chuckled sheathing his stolen blade.

"You've saved the women," he said eyeing her with insight, "and apparently your friend. But you have also sealed your fate as you have revealed yet another chink in your armor," Hana said gesturing. "Someone you care for. Your emotion will be your downfall one day, perhaps when next we meet. But that will be another day.'

Kareta Hana spun on his heels and headed for the ship's gangway, leaping to the decks the final few feet as the ship pulled away from its berth, the plank splashing down into the water. He regained his sea legs and stepped to the rail, looking down. "The next time we meet, Shinobi-San, will be the last."

The ship's horn sounded, and if Hana said more, Kiri did not hear turning her attention to the daughter of her friend. Wincing at the pain in her chest she still managed a tight smile as she started to slowly hoist the girl up. Hana had given her that much respect, naming her an adult, and for some reason that made the samurai smile.

"Easy, Denise," she said grunting, hauling the girl back up onto the docks.

"I have you."

New Year's Day
January 1st, 1937

"Slaughter On The Docks!" Diane Pulitzer read aloud the title banner of the cover story on the morning edition of the *World News*. Diane sipped at her dark coffee, a cigarette smoldering in the ashtray next to her breakfast dishes, omelet and rashers going cold. "Fifteen confirmed dead... Police dragging the river... Kidnapped women rescued... White slavery ring broken..." Diane folded the newspaper and set it aside, picking up her cigarette and taking a puff. "You had a busy night." Suwan nodded.

After she had pulled Denise to safety she had limped off and away into the darkened side streets intersecting the West Side Highway. The police had roared onto the scene sirens blaring even as she had slipped into the shadows and she had felt bad about leaving Denise to deal with them alone, but she could not be discovered. She did not know just how many she had maimed or killed last night, but surely the police would have arrested her, uncaring in the reason why.

The *Shiro* was well under way and heading for the open seas by the time that the police got organized. Ships were called in to pursue, but the steamer was in International Waters and untouchable by the time they caught up. The police did gather up the women however, sending them first to Bellevue to treat their wounds and malnutrition and hypothermia. They would be reunited with their loved ones soon, after questioning.

"Marino will live," Diane said as she stubbed her cigarette out in the glass tray. "The spear wedged in his ribs, the doctors said. He'll be out of action for quite awhile though, using up some well-earned vacation time and sick leave." Diane smirked, shaking her head. "The old man was phoning in his story as soon as he was out of the operating room. Denise will be fine too. She seemed a bit shaken by the whole ordeal when she called but after some rest I think she'll be fine."

"I'm glad," Suwan said sipping at her tea, wincing as she set the porcelain cup back to saucer. Diane and Lancaster had found her limping and bleeding some minutes after the battle, making her way back to the spot where they had dropped her off. Diane had ordered that she be taken to a private doctor that she knew who would ask no questions. Doctor Melton had cleaned and stitched her wounds in her ribs, then removed five bits of shot from her hip and thigh. "He saved the women."

"That he did," Diane said after another sip of coffee. "He had help of course." Diane smiled. "And Hana?"

Suwan sighed. "I have to assume he will return. After the police leave, perhaps by lifeboat. He alluded to grand plans that I doubt he will abandon. But he escaped. I failed again."

"I wouldn't call it a failure," Diane said as she leaned back in her chair lighting another cigarette. "You saved the kidnapped women and stopped his plans. Plus you saved Denise from certain death and for that alone I'll be eternally grateful. You did good."

Suwan smiled, wincing in pain as she shoved her chair back from the table, grabbing up the cane Doctor Melton had given her as she stood. "I'm back to bed," she said hobbling away. "It was a long, hard night.

"You go ahead," Diane said picking at her cold omelet. "Denise will hopefully be back soon with Lancaster once the police are done interrogating her. Then I can hear the rest of the story, right before I ground her for about a year." Diane laughed.

"Go easy on her, Diane," Suwan said pausing in the doorway, glancing back. "She saved my life."

"And you saved hers. Tit for tat, Dear." Diane smiled as she took a long drag from her cigarette. "And Suwan…"

"Yes?"

"Happy New Year."

# THE END

# KIRI ESSAY

I was asked to give a little insight on the creation of Kiri, the Mist, and some background as to how her story came to be. For the full story, I have to go back a few years, so bear with me.

I have always been a fan of comic books, loving the stories and artwork since I found my sister's meager collection when I was still in grade school many, many years ago. From there I learned of Pulp, the likes of the Shadow and the Phantom and so many more, and of course back in the 60's we had The Batman and The Green Hornet on television. Too, I am a gamer from way back in the late 70's, making up characters and stories on the fly. All of that subtly molding me into the person I am today.

I wanted to be part of that culture, to be a cartoonist in the ranks of Marvel or DC, but that unfortunately did not pan out. Eventually I turned my attention and focus to writing rather than drawing. With the advent of the Internet I found an outlet for my creativity, and eventually a website to post the first of my stories. The website was called Restrained Tastes, and the story was Kiri, the Mist.

Kiri was actually my first heroine to find acclaim on the Internet, and her original story is still the longest I have ever written, passing 135,000 words, unfinished. At the time I did not consider her to be a 'Pulp' character, but those who read that original piece said that she definitely was and I had no problem with that, though that was not the initial intention for the character.

The website Restrained Tastes featured stories, articles and images all dealing with escapology, or more directly, Female Escapology. It was there in the site's Chat Room that I first met the webmaster and several very talented writers, all of whom encouraged me to give writing for the site a go. I readily agreed and set out to do just that, though I wanted to do something a bit different.

Another passion of mine since moving to New York was the fascination of old Manhattan and how it came to be. I love the old photographs and reading about the history of the city and figured that I could work that somehow into my story as well. Having plenty of inspiration and hard facts in books, role-playing game source books and the Internet- though this was before Wikipedia, I thought long and hard as to what to write, what character would serve. And it just came to me!

Luckily there was no pay involved because I broke copyright infringement laws right and left. That original story became an episodic endeavor starring some of fiction's greatest characters: Doctor's Moreau and Jekyll, as well as the insidious Fu Manchu. Set in turn of the 20th Century Manhattan, each writing installment ended with Kiri and/or her confidant, Diane Pulitzer bound, gagged and in some type of peril, much like the serials of the old 40's movies. Kiri herself was a Ronin Samurai, hunting the villain that slew her father, master and sensei years before, along with her entire *dojo*, chasing the beast from Feudal Japan to America. I actually have a Western tale with her in old time San Francisco, part of her journey cross country, that has never seen virtual print.

Restrained Tastes has unfortunately closed, so that original story sits on my Hard Drive, though as you have hopefully just read, Kiri has been given life again. Through the help of Derrick Ferguson of Dillon fame, I submitted a story to Ron Fortier here at Airship 27, which he liked but I have to work on. In the interim he suggested I write a short story for this book: MYSTERY MEN (and women) Vol. 3, and of course I jumped at the chance to give Kiri a new home.

I had to update the setting, which was not hard being a fan of old NYC, bringing Kiri into the Pulp 30's. I kept her initial reason for being, hunting the creature that destroyed her life in Japan, and updating her cohorts, keeping Diane Pulitzer and adding a few more, then writing a self-contained short story rather than a serial episode. Ron seemed pleased with the end result, and hopefully you the reader did as well.

I have many more potential stories in mind for Kiri, which will hopefully see print, new ideas and old ones reworked, but regardless, as long as you enjoyed this one, I am happy. I am a storyteller, and I am here to entertain.

CURTIS FERNLUND - was born May 15th, 1962 in Medford, Oregon, which is just a few miles north of the California border. He grew up there with his parents and sister, raised there and went to school, worked and played until 1984 when he loaded a U-Haul with most of his worldly belongings and drove cross country with three friends, eventually settling in Brooklyn, New York. A few years after he met his soul mate, Erica, and moved to Manhattan to live with her where they spent eighteen wonderful years together until her passing in 2006.

Coming to New York City, he was hoping to get a career in the comic book industry as an artist, but had reached a peak in his skill and could not seem to improve enough to surpass it. He turned his focus to writing then, and that in Fan Fiction, as he has always been a comic book fan as well as of the older Pulp genre and a role-play gamer. After dozens, if not hundreds of stories posted on the Internet, another life goal has been achieved, thanks to Airship 27 and Erica, who always had faith in him.

To read more of his work, go to:

http://www.carnaj.com/

# A MAN CALLED MONGREL PT. II

## "And Leave the Rest to Heaven"
### By Derrick Ferguson

The very minute Mongrel returned to the Main Building of the extensive Alternative Technologies complex with the disheveled and exhausted Bonnie Spiteri, Rebecca Henderson went into full mother mode. She'd taken the young girl in hand, personally escorting her to a lower level that was entirely guest quarters and gave instructions to the staff that the girl was to be properly bathed and fed before allowing Sylvester to talk to her. Whoever was in charge of the Infirmary was to come at once and give the girl a full medical examination. And Rebecca further insisted that when the girl was ready that the conference take place in her assigned guest quarters and not in Sylvester's office.

"The poor girl's been through hell, Sylvester. Anyone with two good eyes can see that. The last thing she needs is to be interrogated in that chrome nightmare of an office of yours. Let me get her calmed down, get some hot food into her and let her set a bit. I'll call you when she's ready."

Sylvester Henderson didn't like it much but then again, he didn't have much of a choice. There was no way of getting around Rebecca Henderson once she had her mind set. Mongrel took him by the elbow. "C'mon, bro. Let's go to that nightmare of an office of yours and have a cold one while Ma does her thing."

The brothers walked to the bank of elevators. The top ten floors of the Main Building were reserved solely for the Henderson family and their staff. They all had complete living quarters there even though there was a six acre family compound just a ten minute drive away. But during times of emergency when the safety of the Henderson family could be compromised, Mongrel insisted that they all stay here in the Main Building which was just about as impregnable as he could make it. And as far as he was concerned, with a killing machine as formidable as Cabal running around out there this was just about as much of a time of emergency as he could imagine. This section of the building was restricted to only the family and a handful of trusted staffers all of whom had to be personally cleared by Mongrel himself and were provided with security codes that were changed every five days. A dedicated satellite in geosynchronous orbit over The Main

Building maintained a constant surveillance scan of the entire complex. And the number of security cameras inside the building itself was known only to Mongrel, his brother and a handful of the security staff.

Despite the bright sunshine pouring in through the wide rectangular smart glass windows of Sylvester's office on the top floor of The Main Building, the room felt cold. The many shelves holding numerous volumes of science, philosophy, technology, art and literature suddenly seemed oppressive as thick prison bars.

And yes, Sylvester's office was a nightmare in chrome. He had long ago been teased by his wife and his brother for what appeared to be an obsessive love of the metal as it was everywhere you looked. Their father, Dr. Nayland Henderson refused to set foot in his son's office unless he really had to. He never tired of saying; "I don't see how you can work in there. It doesn't look like an office. It looks like a movie set designed by Ken Adam."

Mongrel headed for the bar to snag himself a cold one. Sylvester went over to his desk, his fingers tapping the surface of his desk which incorporated a fully functional touch sensitive computer interface. Mongrel clinked the two ice cold bottles of Panther Pilsner Beer to get his brother's attention.

Sylvester looked up and impatiently waved it away. "This is not the time to be drinking, Mongrel. We've got a situation…"

Mongrel put one bottle down on the edge of the desk. Took the other bottle, gently slapped it into Sylvester's hand. And just as gently but forcefully shoved Sylvester down into his throne-like office chair. "I know what we've got here. And I know that however it plays out, you and I both need to sit down and unwind a little. One beer ain't gonna kill either of us. Besides, I need to know more about how you know this family and why you said earlier that you killed them. Or were you just being dramatic as usual? Even when we were kids you tended toward the dramatic." Mongrel took a long swig of his beer before continuing with a grin; "That's how come you managed to get away with everything."

Sylvester opened his mouth to speak but was interrupted by a chiming from his office door. He stroked the top of his desk to see who it was requesting admission. He frowned slightly. "This is not going to be pleasant." He tapped the desktop and the door whooshed open to allow the entrance of Dr. Zita Laranjo. Her normally beautiful oval face was now dark with anger and her baleful gaze fixed on Sylvester and she didn't see Mongrel until she was nearly halfway across the office. Upon seeing him, she turned her anger on him with a red-long nailed finger pointing at Mongrel as she snapped, "Thanks a lot for interrupting the ceremonies with your circus act out there! You know how long it'll take to clean up the plaza?"

"Sorry that saving the lives of my family interfered with your television debut," Mongrel replied easily and with no anger whatsoever. In the seven months he'd been working for his brother, he and the volatile Zita Laranjo had seen eye to eye on practically nothing so he had become more than used to her tirades.

"And you're telling me that this situation couldn't have been handled in some other fashion? The news media are screaming for statements and I have no idea what to tell them."

"Well, isn't that why we have a Public Relations department?" Sylvester said. "Let them handle it."

Mongrel sighed. "Sly, Zita *is* in charge of public relations."

Slyvester blinked. "Really? I thought you were in charge of Artificial Intelligence Application Maintenance."

"I was until Mongrel appointed me in charge of Alternative Technologies Public Relations Division," Zita replied.

"Really?" Sylvester's broad shoulders shrugged under the well-tailored black jacket of his Armani suit. "Nobody tells me anything around here." He took a sip of his beer.

Mongrel waved a hand carelessly. "We needed someone with a comprehensive knowledge of Alternative Technologies as a whole and Zita was the best choice."

Zita's mouth opened slightly in surprise and she looked up into the face of a grinning Mongrel. "You didn't even tell your brother that you had me moved from one division to another? What kind of games are you playing at?"

"No games at all. I thought you'd be good for the job. I may have to reconsider that decision since you apparently can't deal with the duties and responsibilities that go along with it. You should be down there handling the press instead of being up here harassing your bosses." Mongrel lifted one eyebrow in a meaningful arch. "And when it comes to playing games, Zita, you got both of us beat. I wanted you where you'd be busy enough that you won't have time to think of some new games. We clear on where I'm coming from or do I have to get real?"

Zita swallowed hard. "Yes. I think I ought to be getting back downstairs. Do you have any suggestions as to what I should tell the press?"

"You'll think of something," Mongrel said smoothly. He waggled his head at the door. "Kick rocks."

Sylvester chuckled as the door closed behind Zita. "Oh, you're going to have fun messing with her, aren't you?"

"You know it. But everything would be a lot easier all the way around if you'd just fire her ass. You know she hates everybody here except for you."

Sylvester shook his head. "I was just as much responsible for what happened between us as she was. Firing her would only compound my weakness. She stays as long as she does her job. I mean it, Mongrel. I don't want you inventing situations just to piss her off and make her look bad. Have your fun but don't hinder her doing her job."

Mongrel eyed Sylvester shrewdly. "You sure you still don't have feelings for her? You did a pretty good job a few minutes ago pretending that you didn't know I'd switched her job."

"Zita needs to be kept off balance. And she needs a focus to fix her anger on. If she thinks that's you, it's better all way round."

"Maybe. But it also might make her think that I'm trying to keep the two of you apart. Which I am trying to do. You've got a beautiful wife who thinks you walk on water and three beautiful kids. What you've built here is a technological empire that will live on for generations long after we're all gone. Don't mess that up, man."

"I won't. You've got my word. Can we get back to work now?"

"Cool with me. The Spiteris. What's your deal with them? You want another?" Mongrel held up his empty beer bottle. Sylvester nodded his assent. Mongrel pushed himself up and out of his seat to go fetch them as Sylvester spoke.

Sylvester took in a deep breath and nodded firmly. "I met Joseph Spiteri maybe eighteen years ago. We were both working for the government at the time. There was a considerable amount of work being done in bionics back then and Joseph Spiteri was one of the most brilliant men working in the field. His work with articulated bioskin armature and integrated neural cognition boosters was some of the most innovative research I've ever seen. We worked together extremely well and it wasn't long before we became friends. Joseph invited me to the family estate several times and eventually he took me into his confidence regarding a long kept Spiteri family secret.

"The Spiteri family suffers from a genetic disorder unique to them. It strikes the males in their family and causes them to suffer from a rapid and horribly painful and lingeringly hideous death that brings on insanity before the end comes. In symptoms it greatly resembles Crimean Congo hemorrhagic fever. There's acute nausea, horrific headaches followed by bleeding of the internal organs and underneath the skin. All accompanied by frightening hallucinations and the feeling that the nerve endings are being soaked in acid. Spiteri men had been known to kill themselves in the first stages of the disease rather than endure its ravages. Joseph showed me recordings made of the few family members who have endured the full stages of the illness." Sylvester shuddered. "I've seen some things in my time, Mongrel...but those images are ones I'll never forget. And they touched me. Joseph asked for my help in finding a cure for his family and I said I'd help."

"When does this family curse strike? What age? Under what circumstances?"

Sylvester shook his head. "It's a strange disease...it can strike at any time and sometimes it will even skip some male members and go on to others. It's a disease that has haunted the Spiteri family for close to two hundred years. I have to admit, I was flattered when Joseph asked me to help. I thought it would be another extraordinary triumph for the great Sylvester Henderson."

Mongrel walked back over to Sylvester's desk and placed the second beer in his hand. "There's no shame in you wanting to help out a friend. Ma and Dad raised us to use our talents and skills in the service of others. If this Spiteri boy thought you could help then it was your duty to do so. But I'm guessing that your finding a cure for the Spiteri family backfired?" Mongrel asked, folding his arms across his chest.

"Mongrel, backfired isn't the word for it..."

"Please, people, please! I'll be happy to answer as many of your questions as I can but you'll have to calm down and ask them one at a time!" Zita was barely able to keep her frustration in check. She hardly expected her first official day on the job to be anything like this.

The sixth floor auditorium was one that had been designed specifically for press conferences and it was filled to capacity. Zita had to admit she felt comforted by the presence of the plainclothes security. The mass of seated reporters shouting questions at her all at once were like nothing she had ever dealt with before. She took a deep breath and said in a voice loud enough to make the speakers squeal. "I mean it, people! Last chance to quiet down or I'll have this auditorium cleared! I'll call on you one at a time!"

At her side, an assistant publicity aide whispered in her ear; "Nobody seated them in proper order. That's why they're so unruly."

Zita frowned and covered the sensitive microphone with her hand while she whispered back. "What do you mean, proper order?"

"They're supposed to be seated in order. Wire service first, then broadcast networks, national newspapers, Internet and Hypernet and finally, regional newspapers. Since nobody seated them, they figured nobody cared." The aide shrugged. "So if nobody else cared, why should they?"

Zita looked at the bright-faced young man with his bow-tie and wide, friendly eyes with interest. An inch or two shorter than herself he looked barely old enough to be in high school. But he must have been exceptional in some manner or he wouldn't have been working here. It was a running joke that at Alternative Technologies even the janitors had Ph.D.'s. "What's your name?"

"Marcelino McGuire, ma'am."

Zita smiled, half in disbelief. "You're kidding."

"Most everybody just calls me Marc. I could help you out with this, ma'am. I've been in Public Relations for ten months now and I pretty much know who's with what and I can call on them for you."

"By all means, do so and let's get this circus over with."

Marc pointed at a plump woman in the fourth row and she gratefully bounced to her feet. "Dr. Laranjo, was this an organized terrorist attack on Dr. Henderson and his family?"

"I have no information at this time that would support that. Next question."

Marc obligingly pointed at a bald Asian man in the seventh row. He gracefully rose and said, "Dr. Laranjo, is there any evidence at all that Post Modern Humans were involved in today's attack?"

"No, not at this time…" Zita lifted slim arms as if to hold back the wails of disgruntled mumblings from the reporters. She was acutely aware that this was all going out live all across the world and she had the sinking feeling that she was coming across as an overpaid, unprepared ass. "…ladies and gentlemen, the attack happened mere hours ago. The investigation by our security staff is still ongoing and you simply just have to give us more time to conduct proper interrogations and corroborate the information given by the attackers."

The reporters honed by years of experience that the hapless Zita simply didn't have immediately pounced on that seemingly reasonable statement. "So then you're saying that the attackers have given you some information then? Have they disclosed their motives for the attack? Was Dr. Henderson and his family the primary targets?"

*"Dr. Laranjo, is there any evidence at all that Post Modern Humans were involved in today's attack?"*

"No they haven't given us any information as of yet!"

"But you just said…"

Zita took in a deep breath and forced herself to get herself under control. She was having no luck at all in trying to control this situation and she had the distinct feeling she was only making it worse. "Listen to me and listen carefully: we have *NO INFORMATION AT THIS TIME* as to who the attackers are, why they attacked or their motivations. I will be holding another press conference in six hours right here and I will have a more complete statement then."

"Dr. Laranjo, who was that man who captured the attackers?"

"That would be Dr. Sylvester Henderson's brother. He's is in charge of personal security for the Henderson family and his official company title is Chief Executive Officer In Charge of Security for Alternative Technologies."

Marc pointed at a frantically waving blond haired man in the first row. The reporter smiled his thanks and stood up. "Is the Henderson family going to request the FBI to step in to handle the investigation?"

"No. They have no intention of doing any such thing. Charalambides Henderson was asked by his brother to join Alternative Technologies because of his years of experience in dealing with such situations as you saw today. Mr. Henderson and his staff is perfectly capable of handling the investigation on his own. And that's it for now. Thank you."

Zita gladly abandoned the podium and motioned for Marc to come with her. "What do you do around here?" she asked, her heels rapidly click-clicking as she walked as fast as she could away from that mob. Marc opened his mouth to answer but Zita cut him off. "Know what, never mind. Whatever it is you were doing, forget it. You're my assistant from now on. And part of your job is to handle those press conferences from now on as well as anything else I don't want to do. You think you can do that?"

"Does a raise come with it?"

"Damn skippy it does. I'll double whatever you're making. And you can look forward to some healthy bonuses as well."

"Whatever you say, ma'am!"

Zita smiled. *Because I'm going to be **very** busy with what I need to be doing…for Sylvester…because if that idiot brother of his or bitch of a wife thinks they're going make a fool out of me then they really don't know me at all…*

❦ ❦ ❦

"You see the cure worked. It was a 100% total success and ensured that the male Spiteri family members would never have to worry about dying from that horrible curse." Sylvester shrugged. "However, there was a price. The cure worked but it made the men sterile."

"Which of course means that the Spiteri family would eventually die out." Mongrel nodded thoughtfully. "Seems like a powerful enough motive to want to kill you."

Sylvester nodded. "Kind of what I was thinking. But why wait so long to make a try at killing me if indeed that's the case and they're the ones who want me dead?

Mongrel shrugged. "The obvious symbolism of killing you and your family on the greatest day of your life. The pinnacle of your success. They kill your family just like you killed theirs. And I could buy it except for one thing."

Sylvester finished off his beer. "That man you fought. The one who killed the family."

"Exactly. He wiped out everybody he could find. The intention was not to leave one single soul alive that could tell what happened."

A chime sounded from Sylvester's desk. He touched it lightly. "Yes, Mother?"

"You and Charalambides come on down. Mirella and Nayland are here with me. The girl says she wants to talk with you."

🐏 🐏 🐏

The guest quarters were as luxurious and comfortable as any five-star hotel. When Mongrel and Sylvester entered, Mirella elegantly stood up and walked over to give her husband a firm hug and kiss. Her wonderfully slim body toned from daily workouts playing volleyball and bowling, Mirella and Sylvester had met and fell in love when she was a Presidential Science Advisor. Her heart-shaped face, framed by tightly curled auburn hair was full of concern. "You okay, baby?"

Sylvester hugged her tightly. "I will be when we find out what's at the bottom of this." Sylvester walked over to where Bonnie Spiteri sat. "I understand you're ready to talk to me, Miss Spiteri. I'm Sylvester Henderson."

Bonnie smiled nervously. "Yes, I know. We've never met but I've heard you talked about so much I feel as if I know you. And of course your family is so well known..." Bonnie looked a lot better than she did a couple of hours ago when Mongrel had brought her in. She had bathed thoroughly and smelled faintly of lavender. She wore a thick white terrycloth robe, fluffy slippers and looked nothing like a girl who had been through the horror of her whole family being murdered. Until you looked into her eyes.

"So what can you tell us, Miss Spiteri?"

"Please, call me Bonnie...as for what I can tell you....it isn't much more than what I've already told Mongrel. Joseph and I were on the patio when we heard the screams and things breaking. He got me to the panic room hidden under the tennis court. Once it locks there's no way to open it for twenty four hours. I was there until it opened and Mongrel found me."

Mongrel took up the questioning. "Has there been anything unusual going on with your family recently? Death threats? Strange people visiting? Any family members upset or worried about anything? Business problems?"

Bonnie shook her head. "Nothing! That's why I can't understand why somebody would want to kill us!"

Sylvester's urgent voice cut in, "Think! There's got to be something, Bonnie. This wasn't a random act of violence. This was a calculated execution. Somebody did it to send a message. Your family must have enemies!"

"Of course they do! Just as yours does!" Bonnie shot back at Sylvester, displaying that hidden strength Mongrel had seen but the others hadn't. "And all your interest and concern in this is starting to make me wonder how deep your involvement is! Maybe my family was killed because of *your* family or something *they* did!"

"Now you just hold on one damn minute..." Sylvester began, taking a step toward Bonnie. Nayland Henderson was quicker and got between them.

"Everybody just go to their corners and take a deep breath," he ordered. Nayland Henderson was one of those men who very rarely raised his voice. Mongrel could count on the fingers of one hand the times he'd heard his father actually yell. But his voice had that particular timbre and authority few men had where he didn't have to yell or shout to be obeyed.

Mongrel felt a familiar vibration in a pouch on his belt and he removed an earpiece, slipped it on and activated it with a touch. He stepped to a corner of the room for some privacy while saying, "I hope like hell this is important, Angie. I got something of a situation here."

In her lavish Chrysler Building office, Angelika Peary replied, "You think I don't know it? That show you put on was something else. The phones haven't stopped ringing."

"Is that all? Angie…"

"No. That's not all and I think you know me better than that. I need you here in New York."

"Angie, that's just not going to happen. I'm hip deep in…"

"Mongrel, the client is requesting you. Not that they don't *all* request you but I think this client fits the parameters of our arraignment. And all I'm asking you to do is come to New York and take a meeting with him. That's it."

"Who's the client?"

"Alfred McCabe."

"Al McCabe? The actor?"

"The same."

"Really? I loved those *Explorers of Infinity* movies he did."

"Who didn't? He's requested a meeting with you."

"Angie, I really can't. Not now…"

"Our contract explicitly states that you must make yourself available to work on high profile cases that will contribute to favorable publicity for the company. This is one of those cases." Angelika's voice softened. "Look, Mongrel, just fly up here to New York and take a meeting with the guy. That's all. If you really don't want to do it after that then I'll take over and work out something. But I can't have you turning down an actor of McCabe's reputation and high profile. We're talking about a man who's been invited to dinner at The White House by the last three Presidents."

"So has my brother but I see your point. Okay, Ange…I'll take a meeting with Mr. McCabe. But that's *all*."

"Thank you."

"Yeah, yeah. See you in a couple of hours." Mongrel broke the connection and turned around to almost bump into Mirella and Sylvester. And Mirella didn't look happy at all.

"No." Her voice was firm.

Mongrel blinked, all wide-eyed and innocent. "No what?"

"I know who that was. Angelika Peary. Mongrel, you can't seriously be considering leaving now with all that's going on here!"

"She just wants me for a meeting, 'Ella. Word. I'll fly up there, meet with the client and fly right back."

Mirella turned to Sylvester. "Well? Aren't you going to tell him not to go?"

"Baby, it's not like he's flying to the other side of the world. In one of our planes he can be to New York in an hour." Sylvester looked from his wife to his brother. "Dad and I can handle the questioning of the men you captured. Go ahead and take your meeting."

"I'll be back as soon as I can. Angie just wants me to be the public face of the company and it *is* the deal I made with her."

"You need to get some sleep as well. You've been on the go for almost twenty-four hours straight."

"I'll sleep on the plane. I'll take Teddy with me. She can fly me to NY and back." Mongrel gestured at Bonnie. "Take it easy on her, okay, Sly? She's been through a lot."

"I'm just trying to make sure our family doesn't go through the same thing her family did."

Mongrel nodded and squeezed his brother's shoulder firmly. He raised his voice slightly; "Dad, Ma? I got to go to New York for a few. Be back as soon as I can."

Rebecca Henderson frowned. "At a time like this? Now?"

"Sly'll explain," Mongrel said hurriedly as he headed for the door. If he let his mother corner him he'd be answering questions for the next eight hours and he was tired enough as is.

Mongrel opened the door and strode rapidly down the carpeted hallway, heading toward the elevators. A breathless voice yelped; "Uncle Mongrel! Uncle Mongrel! Wait up!" The gangly, lanky Tyrell Henderson galloped from around the corner where he had been hiding, all long arms and legs, owlish eyes behind round-framed glasses. He caught up to his uncle and in that half-yell that seemed to be the normal voice of most teenaged boys he said, "When are you gonna teach me how to do what you did to them guys?"

"It's too late. I'd have had to start training you when you were three." Mongrel kept his face serious but inwardly he was struggling to keep from bursting out laughing. "The secret order of ninjas who kidnapped me started my training at the age of three."

"Aw, that's a lotta bullshit," Tyrell grinned widely. "Gramma says so herself when you tell that story."

"How many times have I got to tell you to watch your language? When did I ever give you the idea that you could talk like that around me?" Mongrel suddenly stopped and turned around to glare at the boy. "And why aren't you with your sisters?"

"Aw, they're okay. They're with Mrs. Paroo." Shirley Paroo was governess to the Henderson children. Tyrell's face was crestfallen. "I'm sorry 'bout cussin'...I just get excited, that's all....I forget...."

"Well, don't forget again. I mean it." Mongrel sighed. The so-called progressive attitude of raising children nowadays was one that confused him to no end. Certainly he and Sylvester had never gotten away with using that kind of language in front of adults when they were kids. Mongrel resumed his long legged stride down the wide, quiet hallway.

"I promise I won't forget! Really! I'm sorry!" Tyrell was easily keeping up with his uncle, the only one in the family having the legs long enough to do so. "You goin' after the guys that tried to kill Dad?"

"What makes you think they were trying to kill your father? Maybe they were after me."

"Nah...if somebody was gonna try an' kill you why would they wait until today to do it? I mean, with all the cameras and stuff?"

Mongrel suddenly stopped again, one eyebrow arching. "Y'know, Ty... you got an excellent point there...why would the attackers strike today unless they wanted publicity? And the only reason to want publicity is to take credit. Which nobody has done yet." Mongrel nodded. "I owe you one, boy." He resumed walking.

"Aight! Teach me how to use a samurai sword, then!"

They came to the elevators and Mongrel used a keycard to open the one on the far right. "I'll think about it. In the meantime, here's what you do: you go back to your sisters and stay with them. You wearing the special glasses I had made for you?"

"Sure."

"The first sign of anything funny, you cut 'em on, you hear me?"

"I hear you." The glasses Tyrell wore were a marvel of microminiaturized electronics. When activated the glasses would act as a communications device, transmitting both picture and sound to Mongrel, in effect allowing him to see and hear everything Tyrell did. The elevator came and Mongrel stepped inside.

"You gonna be back soon, Uncle Mongrel?"

"Soon as I can. You want to help me then be my eyes and ears here while I'm taking care of business." The elevator doors closed and the elevator whooshed downward. To a secure sub-section from which a number of tunnels branched off in different directions, like the spokes of a wheel, a dozen in number. Gleaming bullet shaped shuttle pods resting on shiny metal railings waited. There were over fifty shuttle pod terminals exactly like this one placed in strategic locations throughout the Alternative Technologies facility. They came in handy for getting from one place in the facility to another in a short amount of time. The added benefit of it being

*"Y'know, Ty…you got an excellent point there…"*

underground also added yet another layer of security as it meant that one could travel all over the facility without being seen.

The shuttle pod zoomed through a well-lit tunnel toward the direction of a private airfield Mongrel had for his own use on the western side of the facility. He kept a couple of planes there as well as a spacious hangar/workshop where a friend of his kept his aircraft and equipment in shape. The shuttle pod hissed to a stop then rose smoothly upwards on a hydraulic lift until it emerged from the access tunnel into a small terminal. Mongrel stepped out of the pod and exited from the terminal directly into the hangar.

A number of aircraft were parked here and there, some conventional airplanes; others were more experimental in nature designed by Mongrel or his friend. He'd always had a love of aviation and the aircraft he had flown earlier today was one of his designs as well. A number of workmen were servicing the planes, doing routine maintenance or performing upgrades on the avionics or onboard computer systems. In fact, the aircraft he had flown today had been brought here and his friend was personally working on it.

The woman walking around the stubby aircraft, looking at it with a hypercritical eye, was an even five feet six inches tall. The sides of her head shaved bald, she proudly sported a dark purple Mohawk. Razor blade earrings dangled from her lobes. She wore a dog collar around her throat and studded leather bands around her upper arms. The leopard print wife beater and leather vest covered with various buttons of different colors and sizes looked as if they were barely made of enough material to cover her ample breasts. The ear beads of an iPod were plugged firmly into her ears. Despite that, Mongrel could clearly hear the music coming from them: The Sugarhill Gang's "8th Wonder".

Mongrel tapped her on the left side of her head and the woman turned and looked up at him with annoyance. She yanked out her ear beads and yelled, "Don't you know better than to sneak up on somebody like that? You trying to give me a heart attack or what?"

Mongrel reached down to tap the iPod's off button. "You couldn't have heard a charging rhino with this thing turned up the way it was. Aren't you scared you'll go deaf?"

The woman sucked her teeth in annoyance. "That's a big myth. I been listening to music that loud ever since I was ten and the last time I had a hearing test the doc said my ears were so good I can hear some sounds that only dogs can hear."

"And when was the last time you had a hearing test?"

"Wha'd you say?" The woman mimicked hard of hearing, cupping a short-nailed hand behind her ear. Theodora C. Boomer had come to know Mongrel during his mercenary days when both of them were working in Southeast Asia. He was training troops and she was in charge of the motor pool. Mongrel had come to gain a lot of respect for her mechanical ability and when he went to work for Alternative Technologies he knew he wanted her on board to service his vehicles. They'd spent a lot of time in Asia getting into one scrape or another and he was proud to count Teddy Boomer as one of his closest friends.

"How's my Bumblebee doing?" Mongrel asked, walking around the stubby aircraft, checking it himself. "I see you replaced the entire engine."

"Had to." Teddy shrugged. "That fuel you use to make this thing go is so powerful that you actually melted some components by pushing it so hard. Rather than go through the whole thing and pull out the melted parts I thought I'd be better off just replacing the whole damn thing and going through the old engine when I'm bored and got nothing else better to do. "

"Good thinking. I appreciate it."

"I keep meaning to ask you: why do you call this thing The Bumblebee? I'd've figured a macho guy like you would've called it something like The Killer Hawk or The Sky Shark."

Mongrel laughed. "You know anything about bumblebees?"

"They sting and make honey. That's about it."

"They're also not supposed to be able to fly. Their bodies are too heavy and their wings are too small. There's not a thing that's aerodynamic about them. They shouldn't be able to fly worth a lick. But God gave 'em wings and said 'fly' and so they do in defiance of every single law of aerodynamics. Same with this thing here. First time I built and flew it there were bets taken that I'd crash and burn." He affectionately patted the side of the machine. "But ever since I was a kid my mother always told me to do the best I could do and leave the rest to heaven. And that's what I've always done all my life." He patted the machine again.

"Touching story. Full of heart and soul." Teddy grunted. "I'm not sure if I'm supposed to be in awe of your skill in designing and flying aircraft or your God complex."

"I'll let you take your pick. What you got going on?"

"Now? Here?" Teddy threw an arm out, indicating the whole hangar.

"No, Piccadilly Square. Of course I mean here, you nitwit."

Teddy shrugged delightfully soft looking shoulders. "Nothing that needs me to supervise. That what you mean?"

"That's exactly what I mean. You want to take a quick trip to New York?"

Teddy cocked an eye at him. "Last time I went to New York with you we got in a shoot-out at that stadium in Brooklyn. We were just supposed to be going to a Nets game."

"It isn't going to be anything like that. I would fly myself but I could use some sleep. I've had to fly to Louisiana and back and you'd be doing me a solid if you could handle the flying while I grab a nap."

Teddy cocked an eye at him. "I heard about the party you threw today. Sounds like there's a lot going on right here. You really think you should be flying hither and yon?"

"I just went through this with my sister-in-law. I really don't wanna have to go through it with you. You gonna fly me there or not?"

"Hey, hey, you want a pilot, I'm your girl. Don't make me no never mind one way or the other. Gives me a chance to take the Skybreaker out. I've made a few flights in her but just a hop here and there. She really needs a proper shakedown flight." Teddy motioned for Mongrel to walk with her through the noisy hangar toward the airfield.

"So take her for one. What's stopping you?"

"Ah…still waiting on some integrated systems from the Avionics Division. But it's nothing that would keep us from flying to New York. There she is, dude."

Mongrel looked at the triangular blended wing body of the aircraft whose official designation was the X-59. But from Day One Mongrel had refused to call such a beautiful aircraft by such an ugly name. Teddy was the one who had come up with "Skybreaker" and the name stuck. The unconventional aerodynamic shape of the aircraft added to its fuel efficiency and greater range.

"So gas her up and let's get going, shall we?"

*The Island of Zapatero*
*In The Mediterranean Sea Off The Coast of Spain*

Al McCabe watched silently, smoking a Upmann cigar while watching as the gurney bearing the immobile form of Cabal was loaded onto his customized Toshao 1058 ultra-large business jet. With its extra fuel tanks it was capable of making the flight from Spain to New York non-stop. It had the capacity to carry twenty passengers and sleep up to ten at one time. McCabe's plane also had a state of the art conference room with full connectivity, full kitchen and lounge with Moroccan leather furniture. The high-definition video system with full surround sound made viewers feel as if they were in a movie theater. McCabe believed in travelling in comfort.

Professor Devel joined him, a shrimp cocktail in one hand. He rapidly flipped shrimp into his mouth, chewing like a starving man. McCabe looked at him curiously. "How many of those you eat a day?"

Professor Devel shrugged. "This is my fourth. Hey, I like shrimp. I don't complain about you and those obscene cigars, do I?" Devel flipped another shrimp into his mouth.

McCabe shrugged and let it go. He nodded at the gurney as it rose up on the lift into the cargo area. "Is he fully functional?"

Devel swallowed his shrimp before answering. "He is indeed. And this time he'll be ready for whatever happens. I took the opportunity to download a number of martial arts programs into his brain. Vale Tudo, Sambo, Hapkido and a half-dozen others. Whoever runs into our boy is going to have their ass handed to them quick fast." Devel threw more shrimp into his mouth.

McCabe wished the man could eat without all the unnecessary smacking of the lips and slurping. In retaliation he blew cigar smoke at Devel's bowl of shrimp as he said, "Mongrel won't be there. It'll just be his security staff."

"Still, we don't want any surprises do we? This strike right at Alternative Technologies."

"The risk is minimized. I've already diverted Mongrel Henderson to New York. He'll meet me there and I've already made provisions to have him taken care of there. Cabal will take care of the rest of the Hendersons in South Carolina."

More shrimp tossed in the mouth. More chewing and smacking. "Sylvester Henderson is no pushover himself. In his own way he's as formidable and dangerous as his brother."

"But he'll have his family with him. And there's no better distraction. Henderson will be too concerned about his family's welfare to look after his own. Man can't fight effectively if his family is right there with him." McCabe chuckled. "Most men think that their strength comes from family. But it's a weakness, Professor. Only way a man stays strong is to stay by himself. Wouldn't you agree? You're a single man yourself. No kids, right?"

"Wrong. I have two girls. They live with their mother in Budapest."

"You married to their momma?"

"No. I wanted children, not a wife. We have a very satisfactory arrangement. I send her more than enough money to support her and my daughters. They come spend a month with me twice a year. We are all very happy with the situation."

"I commend you." McCabe watched as the loading was completed and the crew chief gave him the thumbs-up. "Okay, time to go. I'll call you from New York, professor and let you know how things go."

"Just bring back Cabal in one piece this time. He represents three years of work and I'd like to get my full use out of him."

McCabe chuckled as he dropped his cigar into Devel's shrimp cocktail. "Anything you say, professor. Anything you say."

Mongrel jogged from the hangar to the Skybreaker. The fueling was all done and the preflight had been performed by Teddy Boomer who now occupied the pilot's seat. She settled a headset comfortably on her head and reached out to switch on various instruments. Hearing Mongrel dog the hatch of the plane shut she half turned in her seat. "'Bout time. I thought you were in a hurry?"

Mongrel held up a huge hero sandwich wrapped in tissue paper. "Had to wait on my eats from the commissary is all. Let's go!"

Teddy obliged by powering up the Skybreaker and it taxied down the runway. Shortly, the plane was in the air, heading toward New York. Mongrel munched on his sandwich, unknowing of the peril to which he was heading into even as an even greater peril headed toward his family…

*To Be Continued…*

DERRICK FERGUSON - is from Brooklyn, New York where he has lived for most of his still young life. He had been married for 28 years to the wonderful Patricia Cabbagestalk-Ferguson who lets him get away with far more than is good for him.

His interests include radio/audio drama, Classic Pulp from the 30's/40's/50's and New Pulp being written today, Marvel/DC fan fiction, Star Trek in particular and all Science Fiction in general, animation, television, movies, cooking, loooooong road trips and casual gaming on the Xbox 360.

Running a close second with writing as an obsession is his love of movies. He currently the co-host of the *Better in the Dark* podcast with his partner Thomas Deja and rants and raves about movies on a bi-weekly basis.

He is also a rotating co-host of the *PULPED!* podcast along with Tommy Hancock, Ron Fortier and Barry Reese where they interview writers of the New Pulp Movement as well as discuss the various themes, topics, ebb and flow of what New Pulp is and why you should be reading it.

Books he had written include *Dillon and the Voice of Odin* and *Dillon and the Legend of the Golden Bell,* which are the first two books featuring his signature character, a charismatic, daring and highly skilled black adventurer/mercenary named Dillon. Check out the DILLON blog http://dillon-dlferguson.blogspot.com/ for more info.

*Derrick Ferguson's Movie Review* and *The Return of Derrick Ferguson's Movie Notebook*T are two volumes of his current reviews feel free to check out *The Ferguson Theater* https://derricklferguson.wordpress.com/

# NEW HEROES GALORE

**M**ystery Men (& Women) has been a joy to produce from its inception as is evidence by this third collection. From volume one, our writers have been eager to accept the challenge of creating new and original pulp heroes. This series has seen the most talented of today's new pulp scribes destroy both gender and race taboos of the past and offer up some truly colorful and exciting new characters.

In this volume, we've two African American battlers. First up is Kevin Noel Olson's World War One veteran turned avenger, the Skein. Then we close the book with the second installment of Derrick Ferguson's newest creation, Mongrel. Doing a serial in an anthology collection with no set schedule was an iffy decision for us to make but after reading this new chapter, we think our readers will applaud that call. Stay tuned as you will certainly be seeing Chapter Three in our very next volume.

Up next is another first in that Greg Gick, harkening back to those old classic pulp baddies who had their own magazines and books ala the Octopus and the Scorpion, has whipped up a brand new pulp villain to take center stage: the Brown Recluse. This is a truly wonderful homage to those fast paced thrillers of yesterday and we fully expect we haven't seen the last of this menacing fiend nor the brave team that battles him.

And lastly, a new writer to the Airship 27 ranks, Curtis Fernlund delivers us a female Japanese Samurai living in New York in the mid-1930s. She is as original a pulp star as you will find anywhere and Fernlund's tale is setting the stage for what we hope will be many more exploits of this exotic beauty known as Kiri.

Of course, as ever, Art Director Rob Davis has provided his usual wonderful illustrations to bring these characters to graphic life and we were truly fortunate to acquire Marco Turini's stunning cover of Kiri for this volume.

There you have it, pulp fans, more new pulp heroes galore. Let us know what you think of this new crew and if you've any suggestions for other types of pulp originals you'd like to see, simply drop us a line. We love hearing from you.  As ever, thanks for your continued support.

AIRSHIP 27 PRODUCTIONS – Pulp Fiction For A New Generation!

*Ron Fortier*
9/24/2012
Fort Collins, CO
(Airship27@Comcast.net)
(www.Airship27.com)

*Airship*
**27**

# Like this book? Here's what's come before...

During the golden days of American pulps hundreds of masked avengers were created to battle evildoers around the globe. *The Black Bat, Moon Man, Domino Lady*, and the *Purple Scar* to name only a few of these amazing pulp heroes. Now in each all-new volume four New Pulp writers introduce to pulp readers brand new pulp heroes cast in the mold of their 1930s counterparts.

In each volume of *Mystery Men & Women* find four brand new action-packed stories starring four original heroes to thrill and excite pulp fans everywhere as brought to you by Airship 27 Productions.

## PULP FICTION FOR A NEW GENERATION!
available at Amazon.com &
at Airship27hangar.com in PDF format

www.ingramcontent.com/pod-product-compliance
Lightning Source LLC
Chambersburg PA
CBHW071240250626
47163CB00001B/270